In *FLIES*, we met the glorious, original and inimitable Noreen Spink (née Purkiss) for the very first time. She won instant fame and instant acclaim . . .

'A WONDERFUL BOOK'
Beryl Reid

'IN SADIE SMITH WE HEAR THAT RARE THING – A COMPLETELY ORIGINAL VOICE . . . RUMBUSTIOUS, FUNNY, MOVING: *FLIES* IS A FIND'
Sarah Harrison

'I ENJOYED IT ENORMOUSLY. IT'S TOUCHING AND FUNNY'
Maureen Lipman

Now, in *DOSH*, Noreen returns to the fray, fighting to keep her man, her confidence, her figure, and noting down in her Woolworth's school exercise books all her deeply philosophical observations of the comic hell of everyday life. Noreen Spink is, quite simply, unforgettable.

Also by Sadie Smith

FLIES

and published by Black Swan

DOSH

The further adventures of Noreen Spink (née Purkiss)

Sadie Smith

BLACK SWAN

DOSH
A BLACK SWAN BOOK 0 552 99439 1

Originally published in Great Britain by Bantam Press,
a division of Transworld Publishers Ltd

PRINTING HISTORY
Bantam Press edition published 1991
Black Swan edition published 1992

This book was set in 12/13pt Melior by
Falcon Typographic Art Ltd, Wallington, Surrey.

Black Swan Books are published by Transworld Publishers
Ltd, 61-63 Uxbridge Road, London W5 5SA, in Australia by
Transworld Publishers (Australia) Pty Ltd, 15-23 Helles
Avenue, Moorebank, NSW 2170, and in New Zealand by
Transworld Publishers (NZ) Ltd, 3 William Pickering Drive,
Albany, Auckland.

Made and printed in Great Britain by
Cox & Wyman Ltd, Reading, Berks.

For Rebecca,
with love

DOSH

I see them both together down the traffic lights today, bottom of our main road; the Pink Panther and his scrawny little tart, that Lollipop. They was stopped there in our Metro with her in my place, the passenger seat. He had his left arm round her, cuddling up and laughing.

Singing.

Traffic Warden come up to them then, one I call Calves, legs like water butts, and he lowered the driving side window to her and the song come out loud and clear.

'Gestapo Jill, Gestapo Jill,
She's out to getcha and she always will!'

Should have known it was him even if I didn't see.

The lights changed then (he must've seen they were about to or he wouldn't of been so brave) and the Metro pulled away with summing like 'ymn strains floating from the window.

Deutschland, Deutschland, über alles . . .

Talk about cocky. That Warden flushed up something chronic. Now she followed his progress through slitted eyes as us Romance authors put it at the same time noting down his number in her little book, pretty toot damn sweet.

Just hope to God she gets him sometime, that's all I can say.

Me – I'd backed into a shop doorway, heart going boom-te-boom at first 'orrible sight of that red car.

Jealousy.

Gee, lousy.

Almost darted out and approached Traffic Warden there and then to give her his name and address, but unfortunately I only knew his name.

Stanley Spink, alias the Pink Panther.

Stanley Spink, out with his tart Lollipop, otherwise known as Sharon.

Stanley Spink, my husband.

Well, after a bit I come out of that doorway and went home, turning into Kitchener Close just as I done a billion times before in fifteen years. It's a better road than most in South Norwood, Kitchener Close, and *Semper Idem*, my home, the first of the white-painted 'Sixties houses to be built there (no open, work-intensive fireplaces, but imitation chimney breast with mock stone cladding), is the best house in the close. Me and Stan saved up for years before we bought it and even then the Family thought we was above ourselves.

Now I got paid-for house and no husband to go

in it, doing things. That front hedge looks as if had bad and very recent perm.

Still, me kitchen nice as always, beams you couldn't tell were plastic, period fitted cabinets, Welsh dresser I got Littlewoods M.O. with Willow Pattern on it very blue in July sunshine with bun feet.

Put Tesco bags down, turned on Radio Two for company.

And this song come on, sung by that busty Yankee blonde.

'Jolene, Jolene,
I'm begging of you, please don't take my man!'

Switched the bloody thing off. And now I full to bursting with the misery of it all. I never been so lonely in all my life.

That Lollipop, laughing in me car . . .

Tears come really hot. Mascara ran.

Then summing, maybe thought of new slim shape, I lost a lot of weight recently, that can't be bad, made me stop and I look in little mirror over sink and see me lashes dark and spiky and thought sod it. Mum always used to say, Think of the bad times when you're tempted to a good wallow, so I think now of the way he was a most unfunny clown in bed for all those years and how I couldn't get no satisfaction like Mick Jagger and how that Lollipop, she can't be getting much either unless he bin studying hard lately, which I doubt.

Felt better.

Turned the radio on again.

At least I got *Semper Idem* and a cat, Fatgirl, daughter of Plum who got run over. And I got

9

lovely daughter of me own and educated son-in-law, Wayne Leech. It was Wayne named *Semper Idem*, always the same in Latin, only it ain't the same, not since that little sleazebag got hold of him. (Stan.)

Used to wonder how I'd feel if I woke up one morning and he wasn't there all warm and hairy in the bed. And now I know.

Still, I was alright until I actually saw them together today, her in the car. Well, sort of alright. Keeping going.

Fed Fatgirl, all quivering and eager (her), put shopping away and picked up pile of new books I got down the library from Miss Sweetbush, our butch librarian. Sometimes I think she fancies me, then IN queue mounts up while her assistant off at tea and OUT queue does the same and she gets ratty, stamping dates harder and faster and swearing when cards won't take on machine and I think, Face it, 'Reeny girl, your morarl must be rock bottom if you thinking about that from her.

Still, she'd saved me two new stories by that queen of Romance, Aurora North-Brightley (false name), A Whore Twice-Nightly, he used to call her, laughing at own joke as always.

Sod him.

I also got out religious booklet HOW PRAYER CAN HELP – should please my dear Sister – and, from further down same library section: FIRST STEPS TO THE OCCULT, MAKING MAGIC WORK, and ALL YOU SHOULD KNOW ABOUT HEXES.

Of course I don't really believe in religion at all, not in *any* system of metaphorical thought, not since my baby Darren died, killed by drunk driver in the Portland Road years ago but you never know.

10

Propped the books up carefully on the settee looking at titles and then went to make strong pot of tea. Put five sweetmeal digestives on Willow Pattern plate.

I hope the rotten sod gets AIDS.

Then crossed fingers, muttered little prayer to God 'n' Jesus that he don't, 'cause if he do I can't never have him back and I decided now I want him, if only to score off of her.

And what Noreen Spink wants she – usually – gets, especially with a bit of help from her friends. That's why the library books, because 'Reeny a bright girl in spite of all they say and fully able to suss out who best to help in hour of need, God or the Occult or Witchcraft or all three together.

Who knows? Always hedge your bets.

So no time for tears now at the thought of slag sitting in my place in the Metro, just pour tea and open books and study. Shan't tell anyone what I'm doing naturally, least of all sister Amy.

But supposing it bloody well works?

Studies interrupted by Amy at back door who would entirely disapprove of these three books. Stuffed them down settee, propped up PRAYER and Aurora's LOVE ALL MY TOMORROWS.

Love all my backside. Why on earth did I pick that up? Old habits die hard, I suppose.

It was then, *then* as I went to open door that the great idea come to me – I would write my own Romance. I mean, I read enough of other people's, those and diet books. Rather write Romance, though.

Amy had cuppa tea but didn't stay long – off down Mother and Baby Clinic, Immigrants don't know English, but that's Amy. He used to say what a good soul she is and so she is but she don't have no real job apart from Roderick at the Water Board and I think all this baby business is suricate. Unhealthy.

Told her to look in at Woolworth's and get me some school exercise books with good stiff covers to them.

'If you're passing, of course,' I added because you should be polite even if it's only your little sister.

Well she poddled off and come back two hours later with the books, also some black biros. Thoughtful.

'So glad to see you're writing your poetry again,' she says smiling.

She don't know.

I ain't writing much poetry these days. Wayne must of told her I did because he caught me once sending off one of my little efforts to *Woman's Weakly*, and when pressed for verdict said it was distinctly after the school of renowned Victorian, William McGonagall or summing. I was no end chuffed.

No. What going down in these little exercise books will be dark and private stuff. Secret. *Urbane.*

'See your next door's sold up,' Amy added casual. 'The Passionate Friends moving out? You'll miss them, I imagine.'

It was Wayne again, named the old dears next door, coupla middle-aged ladies devoted to one another, but then that house never keeps its occupants long, I've noticed. Drains or maybe haunted or summing, I don't know.

The old girls had been nice earlier this year when Fatgirl went missing, her being only a kitten then and blind and all. They couldn't have been nicer if they'd been sexually straight, *he* said.

(She had operation after we found her, something

12

quite simple like nicotine membrane caught on the lower eyelid, now she can see fine, only trouble is getting fat because I thought might as well have her spayed while she at vet's, cat job lot as it were, only no price reduction and he bitter.)

She come in now, clumping through open window, landing on Amy's lap, nearly breaking her bones. (Amy's.) She got up to go.

'Got everything you need?' she asked.

Daft question. Tempted to tell about what I saw down the traffic lights today, then thought not, telling would give it more life, more reality. And I determined that what life it had should be taken away.

'Got more than most,' I said. She thought I being brave. She gimme kiss.

But I have got more than most, including pretty little new granddaughter (who don't have blu-black hair as we all feared like Black Brian at The Feathers, but little whisps of blond, just like her Gramma).

That ain't to say I don't want more. I do.

I want Lollipop's Pink Panther.

I want Stanley Spink.

I want me husband back.

When Amy gone I made 'am sandwich and another pot of tea, then picked up HOW PRAYER CAN HELP, author a painter in France who got religion.

I always thought Hooker's Green was grassy place where prostitutes hang out.

Hmmm. Read a bit then had enough of arty tarty farty and dropped that one and picked up hex book. Hadn't read more'n about a page when feeling come over me this one knew what he was talking about. Yes indeedy.

This chap speaking with authority like Magnus

Magnusson. He said (writer) thoughts are real things. You must always watch what you wish for others because if wish don't lodge with them it comes boomeranging right back there to you.

Strike a light. Remembered how I'd wished him AIDS and, thank God, how I'd reversed it. Read on, good bit about making dolls.

You make a little doll look-alike, then whatever you do to dolly happens to victim on a bigger scale. For example, you cut doll's leg with fruit knife, victim could find his leg sliced up by flying slivers from greengrocer's broken plate glass window.

Interesting.

Still, then we come on to bit about hair and toenail clippings, menstrual blood and semen and that weren't quite nice, also it spoilt 'am sandwich so I put the book away.

Fed Fatgirl, all keen as usual, then bathed and went to bed. Slept raw as weather hot and still slim.

And nobody there to see, a crying shame.

Cheque come from him today again, third one I had, also note asking for water, gas and electric bills for *Semper Idem*. Roderick, who round with Amy in the evening, saw it and said, 'Good old Stan!'

Good old . . .? Nearly hit him with TOMOR-ROWS, which to hand. Hex book would've been better but that right down settee.

Good old Stan?

'He ain't, noway,' I said. 'Don't you say that in here.'

'He'll be back,' Roderick said easily, sinking his chin in his black curling beard. 'Betcha.'

Yeah?

'It's a fact,' Amy said. 'Nine out of ten – er – husbands always return.'

'Well, he can sod off again if he tries it,' I told them, though that just for show. I wasn't letting them know that I wanted him.

'Tell you something, Porky,' Roderick said, stooping to look me in the face. 'I'll have a bet with you that you'll have him back, begging you to take him in, before too long.'

'How long?'

'Before the end of the year.'

'Bloody five months away.'

'So?'

'Oh I dunno,' I said, though I did inside. 'How on earth would we get it all together again?'

'Oh, you would,' my brother-in-law replied. And his black beard waggled and shut up tight round his mouth, making him look very certain.

Times I know why I nearly married him.

'He'll get sick of her before too long,' he went on. 'Trashy little thing like that can't last. Bit of instant rub-a-dub, that's all. More to the point, she'll get sick of him. No offence and all that, but what's he got for her?'

'Wears a little rug,' I said slowly, thinking. 'He's short and fat and old. Well, old for her.'

'Right,' Roderick said. 'Think on.'

Happier. Went up the pub with them. And Dorelia there with Wayne (his perfect mother, the one who does things so well around the house, down on weekend visit, babysitting. I imagine plump pink body in Hilda Ogden pinny. Didn't come to wedding because having histerectomy, lost her husband recently, about the time the Countess, my mother-in-law, died).

D. fit and well now, though when little Janie born she had caesarion and all complications.

Wore my Danish blu cotton top with matching straightlegs and the bit cut out so you can see your watch, new earrings, loadsa plastic beads. Didn't care if mutton dressed up as lamb. Scared stiff of looking like that Thatcher.

Good time in pub. Turbo boost given by Dora saying she wouldn't serve That Couple; Roderick nodding and saying they exiles now, practically everyone in South London give 'em cold shoulder.

People on my side, then? I had wondered. Thought they might be saying Silly bitch, serve her right, letting herself get fat, being too fussy about house, no wonder he went off with fun bint from the train shop. He after perfect models in more ways than one.

Home late and fulla booze.

Woke about four and had to get out to pee. Sat and thought. R. had said, 'What's he got?', meaning Stan, and now I thought miserably of summing I couldn't tell; depends if that slag likes a good big thick one.

Mind, I always thought that Stanley over-sexed and too bloody affectionate by half, but maybe that's how she likes it.

Oh hell.

Over-sexed and always wanting it, but mine.

Not that sleazebag Sharon's.

Got back into bed and lay there watching dawn arrive wondering how it would be if I made tiny straw-haired doll with plasticene pointy nose and matchstick legs and gave her loadsa suffering by sticking in pins and things.

No, no, I thought. Beware the boomerang.

Turned on side thinking I'd have a snooze when

idea come through all clear and simple and straight; it don't have to boomerang at all. Your business, 'Reeny my child, is to make the damn thing stick.

Now that would be fun.

Wicked thing to do though, innit?

Yeah, all part of the (considerable) charm.

Better not do it.

No.

But then again there, I just bloody might.

Monday. Next doors moving out. When the van all packed up and moved away and just their small Mini by the kerb, I asked them in for sherry, being a little bothered I hadn't gone to see Wayne's Mum yesterday, not feeling up to strangers, though I ought.

One would have a drink, one wouldn't because of driving, but both gushed at me in prissy schoolgirl voices that I was too kind.

Racked my brains to think of instant things to say to make amends for weeks of not wanting to know and after a lot of thought took them upstairs to see my new(ish) bedroom festoon blinds in pink-blush, nylon-viscose mixture, co-ordinated valence optional, although of course I got it.

After they'd gone I had another sherry and opened all the windows, place smelt funny. Sat down and wondered idly what they did to one another in bed. Also thought about getting a new job, haven't worked since leaving Piggi's Piazza in April.

Had another sherry.

Housework, gardening. There's a little row of beans, also carrots, spring onions, and four rows lettuces, little ball shape. Why plant them if he set on buggering off?

Sat on settee, closed eyes. Woke to find window

darkened, light all blotted out. Oh shit, I thought, I missed the afternoon.

But no. Big, big van outside and men carrying things in. Noise of trampling feet on bare wood stairs. Shouting and cries.

Peered out from behind net curtains cautiously.

Two teenage boys outside with spots, large amplifiers and a drum kit.

Oh my God.

Thought have another sherry to calm nerves but bottle empty and got splitting head.

Fed Fatgirl and sat down gloomily to think about new neighbours. One of the boys outside no doubt a mate, just come along to help.

Yes, that was it, no doubt.

Fortunately halls adjoin round here. Noise in living rooms too distant usually to be a nuisance. But if they start, if they start up, you go right round there and complain, our 'Reen. Nicely, but that's what you do.

One thing certain though, not going round there now with pot of tea, face full of teeth and welcome. They can provide their own.

All fairly quiet after eight o'clock when van away and evening light come back to Kitchener Close, well, into *Semper Idem*.

And now perhaps house less like its name because instead of two low-profile old maids next door we now got family, with two boys keen to form rock group, well, got drum kit.

Yes.

Still no good rushing to meet trouble halfway. Went upstairs, gave myself huge blast of planet-friendly talc and matching perfume, changed into my Danish blu, put on loadsa lipstick and took off, round to Dorelia's.

Felt in need of telling someone how sorry I am now I wasn't nicer to the Passionate Friends.

Stayed at D.'s last night. Played with little Janie during breakfast, doing piggies with her toes until she screamed. Wayne left house to go to school in bit of a hurry, I thought.

Did ironing for D. for which she very grateful. Not even Mrs Leech the Perfect can turn out a shirt like me, I imagine, with never no tram lines in the sleeves. Purkisses rule, O.K.?

Afterwards me and Dorelia and Janie went up the shops, me with the pushchair. I'd wanted D. to have a great big Silver Cross baby carriage so little Queenie could sit up like Lady Muck and wave at all the peasantry, but this buggy was bought that I can't get the hang of. Double wheels.

Hit things and people. Cannoned into one big bloke on purpose because he yanking poor old dog along. He yelled. Dorelia said, 'Oh, *Mother!*'

Stayed to lunch. D. beginning to wean Janie properly, so was able to weigh in with a good deal of advice. Dorelia listened quietly.

Janie fractious in afternoon. D. said too much attention and playing of piggies but I said nonsense, it's the heat. She thought too might be effect of baby's jab against measles and I said surely not having her done for just childish complaints? And she said rather sharply better than just letting her take her chance.

Filling her with all dead germs? You don't kid me.

Dorelia put on video of THE WIZARD OF OZ to sooth baby who likes to watch the Munchkins. She laugh when they come on. But that's another thing I don't hold with and I told Dorelia, giving them too much TV. Good old-fashioned dummies sooth 'em quicker, I said. Dorelia sighed.

Well, I always rather liked THE WIZARD OF OZ until yesterday. But because Little'un grizzly we had it on seventeen times, at least, the Munchkin bits. I rather got to like the Wicked Witch of the East. She acquired a kind of rarity value in the end.

Stayed for the rest of the afternoon. Wayne come in half past five from teaching English at the Comprehensive. He looked harassed, in fact torn to shreds.

'You need 'oliday,' I told him and he smiled as if he already knew. Still he got six weeks of it coming up even if most of it to be spent attending courses, meetings, organizing visits, background reading, titivating classroom and all the other self-indulgent things them educationists get up to in the holidays.

'Gimme beer for Christ's sake,' he said, flopping down.

Just because he got small bald patch coming at the back like Royalty, kids call him Curly.

He took a great swig of beer and said, 'That's it. I've had enough. I want friggin' out.'

I said, 'Hush, not in front of the baby.' He got up and fetched another can of beer.

Stayed on and on because I was enjoying myself. Easier to put our Stanley to back of mind while playing with little Jane.

About nine Wayne offered to run me home but I look at D. and she say why not stay the night? So I did and they had argument, but I slept all through.

However, I left after breakfast the next day. Thought they might need some time on their own as he broken up (from school). Tact.

*

20

Tuesday. Busy with my heroine, Evelina, a fair scion of her line, got this proud, queenly head burnished with copper curls, incomparably lovely, in great beauty her bosom rising and falling (breathing) in muslin Empire dress at kitchen table. Pens, Woolworth's exercise books all around.

Evelina has a beau, this Duke singularly endowed with massive shoulders, a good leg (two, really), square-cut jaw, strong, clear-cut mouth and piercing blu-eyed gaze from under lazy, laughing lids. He also got hands of steel and irreproachable Michelin lace faultless at strong-cut throat.

Nearly gave myself orgasm writing about *him*.

He all unconscious arrogance, strong profile presented to her while his eyes dance merrily under the brim of his hat. She taps an impatient little foot and lifts a pretty, admonishing finger.

'"*You are all delicacy, sir*," *she said.*

'*Came only a light laugh from behind firm-cut lips. She twinkled up at him . . .*'

Stopped there, remembering lovely, lovely bloke turned up to mother-in-law's funeral some months ago. (Our Stanley nurtures secret hope that he his real father, that I know.)

Scratched out 'square-cut jaw' and substituted 'long, lean, aristocratic face'. Put in 'courteous brown eyes' instead of 'piercing blu'.

'*Evelina stuck there, twinkling up at his long lean aristocratic face, listening to his every word with big round eyes.*'

Stopped again because feeling something not quite right. Then laughed at silly self as see anatomically impossible. Scratch out 'eyes' and write in 'ears'.

Still something not quite right. A bit extra needed here, perhaps?

'She gave great head.'

Still undecided. Not entirely sure just what that means though I seen it printed in a paperback somewhere so it must be right. One of them Hollywood books, the sort Wayne reads on holiday.

(Told him recently about writing Romance and he said, after a few beers, 'Outline your plot to me.' 'Plot?' I asked him, 'What's this plot?' My characters just get together and do lovely things.)

But back to work.

'The Duke, who was obviously of the Quality and whose Michelin lace sat so irreproachably at his strong-cut throat, bowed with consummate gallantry. She was as pale now as she had been red before. He pressed himself ruthlessly to her soft and quivering lips . . .'

Ooh, you never was a demon lover, Stanley Spink, and now this set me longing in a whole new way . . .

Ha! Chance'd be a fine thing. Forget it. Still I can write about it even if I ain't getting any, right? So that Evelina really hot for Duke.

'In spite of the heat of the Assembly Rooms she shivered uncontrollably, an agonizing, sickly fear gripped her and she knew a moment's impulse to stiffen in sudden apprehension. By the fitful light of the moon he could see that she had a dusting of freckles across her exquisite face, the one with the tip-tilted nose and eyes.'

(That's after they gone outside of course, he sees them.)

I was just having them get into a magnificently appointed carriage drawn by six powerful matching bays with crested door panels when the noise began next door.

Fatgirl, who had been sleeping in a round blob down by my feet, fled incipiently upstairs. Later found her crouching under bed, place where she'd been born, only one in the whole house she reckons really safe.

They can't have much reason, cats, well they got different logic. I mean, if it's raining when she goes to one door she always tries another one, all hopeful. You can see her thinking Maybe it ain't so bad out this one.

Always is.

Now I could have told her noise coming through wall of very room she hiding in, one she supposing safe.

My heart sank. It means new boys got bedroom next to mine.

There was symbols going and drums, and they were playing to a particularly noisy tape. Didn't know the group and didn't wish to. Went downstairs again and sat at kitchen table.

Evelina and her Duke suspended in time outside Assembly Rooms, but noway could I concentrate with that row going on. Then happening to lift me eyes to window I see her go out into back garden with orange plastic basket full of washing and begin to hook up clothes line. Now me chance.

Went out.

'Hullo!' I said and flashed the Purkiss teeth.

She glanced up briefly, mouth full of pegs. 'Oh, 'ullo.'

'My name's Noreen,' I told her. 'People call me 'Reen.'

'Oh?' she said, pegging.

I waited.

Nothing.

'You just moved in,' I told her. Silly. She knew that.

She nodded.

I waited.

Nothing.

Just opening my mouth to ask if she fancied a cup of tea when a toddler appeared all unsteady in the open doorway behind her, climbed laboriously down the step and squatted on his haunches on the path.

Filling his panties by the looks of things; concentrating hard and going red. Then he stood up again all happy. I saw he'd picked up an earthworm while he'd been down.

She turned round and caught him then, *whirled* on him, face livid, almost as if she enjoying it. Left the line sagging, shirt-arms dangling as she strode across and grabbed him by the arm.

'What you doing 'ere?' she shrieked, and smacked his hand. Poor little fella dropped his worm and looked up all dismayed. 'That's dirty!' she screamed. 'And if I find you done a poo . . .' She was yanking him into the doorway. 'Get inside. I can see I'm gonna have to wallop you.'

The door slammed shut. I heard the kid wail and I stood 'orrified. I mean, she was vicious.

I went slowly back indoors. Right, lousy bitch, I thought. I got your measure. No cups of tea. And if I hear child scream or even wail a lot, I'm ringing N.S.P.C.C. toot sweet.

After about an hour the rock noise upstairs left off and I settled at the kitchen table again and picked up pen.

But summow Duke and Evelina lost all their appeal.

Went down the Job Centre today and saw her on the other side of the road. She saw me too but didn't smile or anything, just ignored me. She got one of those permanent faces, thin, fed up and never changes, mouth always down in sort of grouch.

She was pushing the little boy in a chair and he was crying, rivers of snot hanging from his nose. Outside Marks I saw her park the chair and hit him. Bound to make him stop crying, that was.

Nothing I fancied in the Job Centre or perhaps I was too distray. Seems wrong that those who got baby boys don't want 'em while those that do watch 'em die in car crash on the Portland Road. He'd be nearly thirty now, my Darren, Dorelia's big brother.

Went home and called Dorelia to make sure Jane alright.

'You wouldn't never slap her if she grizzled in the street?'

'Oh, Mum!' she sighs, all impatient. 'Of course I wouldn't. I'd beat her to death with bars of iron.'

Put the phone down smartly on her. Annoyed. She no right being flippant. Shall speak to her *very crisply* when I see her next.

Toyed with idea of charging round then and there but remembered Wayne home for the holidays and thought maybe he like to get outside a few Hollywood books and cans of beer without mother-in-law around. I can be a perfect model of tact at times, and quite amaze myself.

Got out the Duke and as if on cue as us writers say, noise started up next door. Baffled and furious. Is this to go on all the summer holidays?

Enough to make you think of moving house. Not that I ever would. But enough to start you wondering how it would be to live in one that wasn't semidetached. I reckon it'd be strange.

Yeah, strange. Nice, though, in some ways.

Strange.

But nice.

You never heard the Passionate Friends next door, too busy doing quiet saucy things to each other, shouldn't wonder. And her before them, old Natural Substances, thought that P. G. Wodehouse such a gift, you never heard her either. Well, reading don't make much noise.

But you can hear this new one all the time. Always yelling. Summing always wrong, usually little boy.

'Come out me saucepan cupboard, you little sod!'

'You eat it all up or you don't get no more today!'

'Up to bed, you little shit, I'm sick to death of you!'

Not 'alf as sick as I am of her and her shouting. The usual complaint is 'I'm fed up of you today!' – as if little kid doing something new and rare and awful every day. I listen hard for sounds of real ill treatment case I have to call N.S.P.C.C. but so far the rough stuff mainly verbal.

Bad enough.

Only one of the big boys is at school. The other's older – and half daft if you ask me, definitely a few pence short of a shilling. Mooches around all day with big black hat on, hands in pockets. Never speaks. Never does nothing much, not even blink his eyes.

I've nicknamed him Bonzo. The younger one I call Skinny. He got mean little narrow slitted eyes like Traffic Warden. Haven't seen Daddy yet.

Poor little *Semper Idem*, having that bunch next door!

Note through the post from Stan, all formal, addressed to Mrs S. Spink. He says can he come and see me?

26

Showed it to Roderick and Amy.

My dear sister said at once let him come, be an opportunity to talk things through. I suspicious, they always doing that on EastEnders, never get far. Besides, he'd be lucky to make himself heard above the row next door.

Roderick abdicated absolutely neutral ground.

Amy said I owe Stan a bit of talking because I'd packed his case for him when I found out about that Lollipop. Puzzled over this for minutes and finally told her she was mad.

Still, I thought about what they said. I need that Amy though I don't usually tell her because she younger than me.

Up the shops about four hoping meet Wayne and Dorelia. Wore my Danish blu. Got magazine – I like that Claire Rayner, says life too short to diet, not like that Miriam Stoppit, a right old killjoy she is.

Brooding. Don't think anything will bring Stan running until he busts up with this tart. Remember with brief joy how I pulled her hair out in that dirty caff last April. Sigh! That was living.

Going home. Skinny and Bonzo on other side of main road just before our close, with mates. Skinny said summing out the corner of his mouth and there was laughter as they looked across at me. Ignored it.

Went in and found another note from Stanley, marked 'By Hand'. Oh, let the bugger sweat.

Made large pot strong, strong tea.

Eating sweetmeal digestives and reading in Claire Rayner how if annoyed you should hit cushions really hard to get rid of all your aggro. Blimey, I should have no cushions left.

Finished magazine. Eaten all biscuits in house. Cheesed off.

'"I am fed up of shadows," said the Lady of Shallot.' (Tennyson.)

Oh, why can't the Duke step right out of the Woolworth's exercise book, bow with exquisite courtesy and carry me off with lazy, laughing gaze? Because this is real life, this is, and there's only short, fat Stanley Spink, laughs when he farts in bed and shouts 'Earfquake coming!' And there's the savage bit next door, too, got dear little baby boy she hits when mine been dead for years . . .

Of course life is Dorelia too, so pretty and sweet, got straight legs and talk about bright – got to the Grammar School and could have gone on *anywhere*, except she married Wayne on account of . . . well, never mind about that now.

And of course there's little Jane.

And Amy.

Went out into the hall and rang her, batting her ear for half an hour and running up bill for Stanley.

She said advice Claire Rayner gave is very sound.

That Bonzo just isn't right. He never speaks, and he's so pale, wouldn't come as news to me that he had 'eart.

He's with the boys but not one of them. They got girls, hang around on the corner with them, slaggy little pieces with their tops unbuttoned. Bonzo don't have a girl and nobody speaks to him. It's as if he wasn't there.

Several bricks short of a load.

Went out into back garden to check beans. Watered lettuces because no rain. Wonder about the ones up the allotment – perhaps he waters those.

Then went to look at gnomes and found empty lager can floating in little blu pond. Fished it out and then saw one of the gnomes had top of his hat broken off. Found the red tip lying in the grass beside a stone. Who would have thrown summing at them harmless gnomes?

Sad.

This morning found spray paint on caravan, no words, just loops as if someone gone wildly round and round. Looks as if aimed from top of alley wall. Also more lager cans in pond.

Fetched white spirit and cleaned van. Then did inside with curtains pulled.

Later went up D.'s and played with baby, then down the clinic to meet Amy. Didn't tell either of them about damage to the garden; Kitchener Close select and residential (was) and I feel dirty and ashamed.

All four of us out on Amy's patio with D. taking photographs. Then Amy tell me Stanley been on phone to her at work.

'What's he want?'

'Just to talk to you.'

'Why didn't he ring the house?'

'I think he feels a certain reticence.'

He'd feel a certain back-of-hand if I could get at him. Fancy bothering Amy down the Clinic, the little toad!

Dorelia very obviously not looking at me, busy with little J. — but I was past the stage of trying to act all nice about her father. Events speak for themselves.

'Not after a divorce, is he?' I said to Amy sharply before I could stop, voice rising even though I didn't mean it to.

'Oh, I don't think it was that at all,' Amy said gently.

But all the same I was aware of nasty cold feeling

of chilling wind begin to blow, I felt it before, then when he started paying bills and sending money it fell away.

Everything's changing. He's gone, *Semper Idem* not the same since that family of scarecrows moved in next door . . . Help me, someone. I'm frightened.

Didn't say anything aloud. Took baby from Dorelia and bounced her on my knee. (Baby.)

'I dunno,' I said to Amy, holding the baby close and burying my face in her sweet-smelling little neck. 'Don't think I know anything much these days anymore. Might ring 'im at work if I ain't got nothing else to do.'

And I might not.

Wayne sent over by Dorelia with photos taken on Amy's patio last week. It's no use sending them through the post; you put *Photos don't bend* on envelope and they arrive with *Yes they do quite easily, see?* written underneath.

Wayne saw THE DUKE AND EVELINA lying on the kitchen table.

'Hey, hey, hey!' he said and bent over it, his chest medallions swinging out and clinking. Usually they lurk hidden in the dense curls on his chest, Pisces the Fish, George the Dragon and so on, but they get obvious when he excited. 'What's this?'

He lifted my pages all unasked and riffled through them.

'A perfect pastiche,' he said at last, dropping them, and I just *glowed*, him being a proper English teacher and all.

'Any suggestions?' I asked him, trying to sound humble.

He thought hard.

'Needs a bit more pizzazz,' he said after a while

as if that all, only a small thing needed. 'You could try putting some raw sex into it.'

'No, no, no!' I cried. 'That's the whole point about the Duke – he doesn't *have* sex.'

'What is he then,' Wayne asked, sounding genuinely puzzled. 'Some kind of soaking wet fairy?'

I explained about the Duke being romantic and that Evelina a virgin – and likely to remain so with all the din from next door.

Wayne nodded understandingly. I'm lucky in my son-in-law. And when he'd gone I tried pizzazzing up the Duke.

Not satisfied.

I mean she could feel his male hardness through his exquisitely tailored breeches at a pinch but if he crushed her salt flesh to him it would ruin his Michelin lace I said so irreproachable and faultless.

'*Above the faultless, irreproachable points of the lace at his strong-cut throat their probing tongues were furiously entwined . . .*'

No, no, have a heart, it just don't go, anyone can see. Wayne bin reading too many of them Hollywood novels. Sex, sex, sex. I never met a man who didn't think about it all the time.

Mind, this little girl thinking about it pretty often these days too. Funny how you come to value something when it's not on tap.

Bit like that old Wicked Witch of the East, these days, is sex. Rarity value.

What's a girl to do?

I seen Big Daddy now.

I was ironing inside, listening to Radio Medway where there was this disc jokey, phoned this birthday girl who at 'otel in Dover. Going to give her birthday message from her parents and play request.

31

But it come out that she having dirty weekend in Dover while her parents thinking she off with a party of friends; she tells all before the dj can stop her.

'Hem!' he interrupts her, embarrassed. 'You do realize you're on the air?'

Silence. Of course she didn't realize, she must have imagined it was a close pal calling her or summing.

'Can you describe the view out of your window?' he rushes on, high and nervous, chatting to fill awful silence she just made.

'No, I can't, I ain't had any time to look out yet,' she answers, then gasps at what implied by what she said.

Laugh? I nearly died. And died and died. (Though in spite of awful cockup I'd have changed with her.) Then laughter cut off abruptly as I happened to glance outside. Through the window I can see Scarecrows cutting down lilac tree.

That tree props up the boundary fence and most of the trunk is on our side. We got a patio there, handy for drinks and barbies, nice shady place in summer, sort of enclosed. I used to say to him trim the lower branches, make it a bit tidier, but he never would and I saw that he possibly right.

And now these Scarecrows at it with a buzzsaw, or about to be. Maybe I just in time.

Dad had a monkey face, street crafty, looked like he'd give any secondhand dealer a hard time. Sexy in offbeat, macho sort of way, maybe he put it about and that why she permanent and bitter.

Not that I was bothered about that. I run out, waving me arms and shouting.

'Leave it alone! You can't do that!'

He didn't miss a beat. Well, he must of known

that I'd be out. Cutting that tree, he was expecting it.

'I just did,' he said, throwing a small branch on to our side. 'Do yourself a favour, lady, and don't shout. You get up there,' he said to Skinny, who was beside him. 'Take the 'andsaw. I want them little top ones off.'

'What you think I got, bleeding wings?' Skinny retorted, but he got going and began to climb.

'Perhaps you'd care to borrow a ladder?' I asked all sarcastic.

'Yeah – hop off quick and get one,' he said, not taking his eyes off Skinny.

'I hope you realize that's a party fence!' I shouted. 'And that lilac's a party tree!'

'Hang about and you won't be bothered by it much longer,' Dad said.

'Then we'll 'ave a party!' Skinny shouted down.

'But I want that tree left as it is!'

'Too bad,' said Dad, platonic. 'It's dangerous. Roots at the foundations.'

'Oh, please leave it!' I called out.

'Don't be bloody daft,' Dad said, and Skinny shouted something down like 'Piss off, Ma!'

I went back indoors all sad and sentimental. That tree lovely in the spring, especially evenings.

For hours after that it seemed I heard the rasp and whine of the saw while the branches crackled and fell down. Most landed our side – no doubt the Scarecrows saw to that. They certainly didn't try to pick them up.

Fatgirl stayed upstairs under the bed all day but later, in the evening when things quieter she come out for her tea and then she and I went out the back door and stood looking at the scene.

Garden looks naked and all different, gone back

33

to boxy little L-shaped plot of fifteen year ago. Cara still in its place, also Stanley's bean sticks, but me little blu pond all dried up from heat and the Red Gnome still sitting with his hat knocked off.

Picked up Fatgirl and went in and shut the door. Usually she likes to wander at this time of night but I'm thinking she'll be safer indoors. There could be anything out there, menacing and 'orrible.

Oh, poor, poor, poor little *Semper Idem*.

Saturday. Went down D.'s. Wayne in a good mood and asked after progress on THE DUKE. Told him I hadn't had the energy lately. Wasn't going to tell about the Scarecrows, but D. noticed I was down.

'It's the house,' I said. 'We got these new neighbours. I did tell you.'

'Aren't they nice?'

'No.'

'How not nice?' Wayne asked.

So I told about the rock music and the little boy and the tree and they both listened.

Wayne said, 'We'll walk home with you, Ma.'

I said, 'Janie should be asleep.' But D. come right back with she'd sleep in her chair. Didn't argue. It's nice when people care that much.

Kitchener Close quiet as the grave as we approach. It would be. Wayne and Dorelia wondering what all the fuss about no doubt. We all went in, had a cup of tea, but still the noise didn't start.

However, once they'd gone of course, it did.

Could of *howled*.

And then I remembered that Claire Rayner.

Stood up, piled all the settee cushions in a heap, even me frilly scatters, then hit at them with fists. I smacked those cushions six, silly and sideways till they was plumped up past belief, as they'd never been plumped up in their lives before. I was red in the face as I paused for breath – and then I went at it again, wondering if they could hear me in next door.

Daft ha'porth. What a thing to worry about.

Pounded on, gasping out, 'You buggers, buggers, buggers!' – but for some strange reason it weren't Skinny or Dad Scarecrow I had in mind or even her with the thin lips. It was Bonzo's great pale moonface I saw printed on every cushion. I hit his face, all weird and silent under his black hat, a hundred times or more, easy, must have been.

Then I sat down breathing, couldn't do no more. But I felt much better, really really did. I'd smashed his face. I'd do another member of the family tomorrow.

Went to bed.

Woken about two by wee-wee of sirens. Police cars down in the main road I thought, but they come up Kitchener Close.

Got out of bed to look. Ambulance down there and blu-uniform men running into house with apparatus. Awful commotion going on next door.

Then double quick their front door opened and out all come again only this time Bonzo between them on a stretcher. Face the colour of paper in the light from the sodium lamp. His eyes were closed tight shut.

I knew. God help me, second time I see dead body within twelve months.

Then old Mother Scarecrow come out of door and I see she was crying. Funny to think of someone crying over Bonzo.

Ambulance went off with great deal of noise but I knew it weren't no good. He'd be D.O.A. on arrival or my name ain't 'Reen Spink.

35

Got back into bed again, shivering and thoughtful. Couldn't sleep.

About five got up and dressed and went round Amy's.

Back home again now, writing this.

Amy in her wisdom tried to make me see absolutely no connection between me hitting cushions and that Bonzo dying. But Roderick, speaking plainly as usual (I think he was ratty at being woken up so early), said he for one had always believed in sympathetic magic.

Just what I had worked out for myself.

Those cushions acted like a hex doll. I got no need to make one and stick in pins. I'd hit Bonzo. His face was on every cushion. And he'd died.

'Nonsense!' Amy said, sounding just like our Mum. But as she finished that very word, the dog raised his head in a corner of the kitchen where he'd been asleep and howled. Eerily.

And Roderick and I turned and looked at one another.

'Well, if he weren't dead before, he is now,' said he, all matter of fact, and we nodded together. He and I, we got this Celtic blood. His granddad a 'ighlander and though the Purkisses have been Cockneys for generations out of time, Gramma Purkiss was an O'Kelleghan by birth and come from southern Ireland. I get admonitions. And I seen ghosts three times, not always when I wanted to.

Went home after Amy gimme breakfast. Kitchener Close all silent, some got curtains drawn. No rock music today. Bonzo dead.

And oh God, part of me rejoicing and part of me afraid of what I done — not that anyone's going to know unless our Roderick tells – and third and apprehensive part wondering what next gonna come in from next door? For I can feel the evil of the Scarecrows somehow seeping through the walls, right into *Semper Idem*.

Monday. Worked on THE DUKE, pondering again whether to give him balls and have him slam into the heroine, Hollywood style. But come to same conclusion – tasteless. Also up against truth problem here – they wouldn't have done it before marriage, would they, being of the Quality, and not like Stan and me, affectionate.

But then again, if I had them being affectionate after marriage, would there be what Wayne calls box office in blow-by-blow account of married love? I mean, nobody really wants to know what happens afterwards. Cut the domestic bliss, I feel. Ours certainly weren't all that much to write home about.

A real problem here. I dunno what to do. Sat chewing biros for a bit, then suddenly scrunched up all rude pages and binned them. Writing is too much like hard work.

Cleaned house, washed hair. Applied lemon-coloured facepack and stood at bedroom window frightening anyone who looked up from the street. Huge blasts of White Satin, then off down the library to take magic books back to Miss Sweetbush.

Slack time at the library. Miss Sweetbush sniffed the air, then leered at me, monocle jiggling gently. Ignored her.

Home with just library card in my hand. Sat down at kitchen table again, rested head on arms. Bloody White Satin all around.

Feeling randy and wanting it. Time going by and nobody getting younger and soon there'll be a last time for it because sooner or later a last time for everything in this poxy world.

And what's me due and belongs to me is far away, or as good as.

Oh hell, what a mess.

Fatgirl jumped up on table (poor table) and gimme a cupboard-love nose touch. Wiped off nose touch and fed her.

Then on Celtic impulse left house, climbed on passing pay-as-you-enter single decker bus and before I knew it was stood in Lewisham by terraced house and seedy, cheap shop turning off Lee High Road.

Outside that five-star Egon Roany place, Kay's Pantry.

Old-fashioned doorbell tinkled as you went in. Had to hold on to handle because place all green after the sunny street and looked as if time warp ahead and I might need beaming up. I mean, black-apron waitress, red check cloths on tables, canework chairs. Joe Lyons used to have those in the 'Fifties.

When your eyes cleared, however, you could see sauce stains on the cloths and ash in white sugar bowls and cruets all bunged up with gungey pepper. God it was a dump. They hadn't heard of healthy eating here and wouldn't, by the look of things, until millenium come. They hadn't even heard of basic hygiene.

Didn't know what else I'd find, summing even nastier perhaps, like crummy little bitch with frizzy hair, long nose and whiny voice, our Stanley's dearest Lollipop. All I knew was I'd come in here for something.

And then I saw him, sitting on his own towards the back, untouched cuppa tea in front of him.

My God he scared me. Seemed to have shrunk

somehow and all in upon himself. He looked smaller, thinner; had his pipe out though he wasn't smoking, staring straight in front. Didn't even look up when the shop door opened.

Waiting for her after work. But if that so, why didn't he look up? Why sitting there so still and hopeless looking?

I went over to him without meaning to. He looked up indifferent.

'Oh, 'ullo, 'Reen.'

''Ullo, Stan.'

It was as if we met for first time since this morning, not after gap of months.

'I got your letters.'

'Right.'

'Siddown, then?'

'If you like.'

Same old reply. I sat. Waitress come hovering up, blasted nuisance, but there was nobody else in the place, hardly surprising, and we got all her attention.

Ordered some tea to keep her quiet.

Bit embarrassed now (me) and wondering why I come. Heart beating all nervous, thinking he'd think I was chasing him. Then I thought sod it, feeling annoyed. He was the one who should be embarrassed.

'Well?' I asked him when that waitress gone.

'Well what?'

'How you bin?'

'Alright.'

But he wasn't alright now, there were tears on his face, and I couldn't remember the last time I see Stanley cry. Most likely when someone kicked over a pint of Worthington at one of our barbies.

39

Pretty soon there were two cooling cups of tea between the two of us.

'You come out here to gloat?' he asked suddenly.

'Should I have done?' I said surprised.

'Thought you might of.'

He banged old tobacco out of his pipe. I saw his hands were shaking. Bloody hell – he looked like old, old man.

'She give you up or what?' I asked direct.

'Something like that.'

'Permanent?'

'You could say so.'

'Tell me.'

'No.'

I shrugged.

'She didn't like me paying bills on *Semper Idem*,' he said, it all coming out in a rush. 'Said there was only so much money in the world. She done it all before, see?' he went on bitterly. 'Had a married man.'

'Prat. Didn't really think you was the first?'

He looked foolish, silly. Picked at a loose thread (there was plenty) in the tablecloth.

'And then when Dorelia brought the baby round . . .'

'Ooh, she never! She wouldn't! Take little Janie to see . . .'

'No, no, no. Dorelia thought Sharon was out. It was me she come to see. Well Sharon was out, I told Dorelia so because she wouldn't have come else. But Sharon saw her and come back on purpose. She was jealous, well she didn't like Dorelia visiting. They knew each other from way back. "Still touting it around, I see," Dorelia says to her.'

I began to feel warmer. My lovely, lovely girl.

'Well then Dorelia began packing up the baby

40

– they don't half have a lot of things these days – and Sharon says summing about they might as well try to get on as she was going to be her stepmother. It was the first I'd heard of it. I was just beginning to see then she might be after me money.'

'What money?'

'That's when Dorelia smacked her across the face. Told her she must be out of her mind.'

My daughter! My beautiful daughter! What a chip off of the old block. One way and another, that tart suffered quite a bit of violence at the hands of Spinks.

'Then Sharon says she see Dorelia only just got married in time and Dorelia replies at least she got her own husband and then, to me, don't expect to see her or the baby again while I'm living with this . . .'

'Gross little scumbag whore.'

''Reen!'

'A spade's a spade. Mind, in this case, it's bloody shovel.'

'Yeah, well.'

He tried to light his pipe. Logic got him there. Men of his generation, all women who give it away are whores.

'She wasn't a whore to me,' he said after a bit. 'I can't get nobody to understand. She was my beautiful Sharon.'

'She was whore,' I told him. 'Leave it out. You and your fantasies.'

Logic got him again. He knew well enough it was the idea of her he'd been after; the long, long legs, the (I suppose) randiness, the youth.

'I must've been mad,' he said, groping for his handkerchief, for something had set him crying

41

again. 'I knew what she was, blimey, I could *see*, but I kept on hoping it wasn't so. I kept on hoping.'

'Story of your life,' I told him, thinking of time he ordered cabbage seed from well-known garden centre and we got sea kale come up, monster plants we didn't want. 'Blow your nose.'

He trumpeted, a sorry figure, broken down and empty for loss of a sweet dream. I don't know when I've seen anyone so low.

'After that,' he said, starting to put the handkerchief away, 'it was all money, money, money.'

'Keep it where you can see it,' I said. 'In your hand. That's the handkerchief.'

'Hush, 'Reen,' he said, looking round – and that's when I knew he was improving. Telling me things had helped him. A few careful comments of the type he's been used to for thirty years and hadn't been hearing lately, that was what he needed.

'It all come down to money in the end,' he went on sadly. 'I knew, even though I thought – I mean I hoped it was . . .'

'Your body she was after?'

'Yeah.'

'Don't kid yourself,' I told him sternly. 'You look like cross between pocket Orson Wells and Mickey Rooney, it has to be your money that they're after.'

'I never thought I was Clark Gable,' he said, nose in air.

'Oh? She tell you you was Leslie Howard, then?'

He sighed. 'She's never even heard of Leslie Howard. And that was another thing.'

'Yes, I can see that would make a big division.'

'No, 'Reen, the age gap. I was worrying about me lettuces. And she thought that was *funny*. Summing old codgers did, she said.'

'Well?'

'Did you water them, the ones I planted in the garden?'

''Course I watered them. I got nothing else to do, had I and all I could think of, naturally, was whether them lettuces was alright. God it nearly drove me mad, worrying about them lettuces and how they might be drying up. Them and the baby beans and all.'

He didn't even notice it was sarcasm.

'I did the ones up the allotment, see,' he went on. 'I mean, we haven't had much rain. Are the beans very high this year? Up to the top of their poles yet?'

'Oh, Goddamn your bloody sodding beans!' I shouted, and that brought the waitress at the gallop, stupid face puckered in enquiry. We asked for two more teas and she removed the dead ones gingerly.

'What you doing here, anyway?' I asked him. 'Hoping she'd see the light and come running back to tell you she like lettuce a lot after all?'

'No,' he said. 'I come here to see if I could remember what I saw in her.'

'Her long legs, I suppose.'

'No. She laughed at my jokes. Well she did at first.'

'She ain't heard them billion times like I have. But she will, Stanley, she will.'

'No,' he said simply. 'Never again. No more. Bloody hell, Mog. I told you we split up.'

'Don't you Mog me, Stanley Spink!'

He sighed again and fiddled with the cloth thread, not that it made much difference to the cloth. I reached out and smacked his hand to make him stop.

'We only had this one room above the shoe shop,'

he said, still fiddling. 'And when she told me to get out, I went. I bin sleeping in my allotment hut.'

'Needs her room for her trade in bitsa oofy rough, I suppose.'

He shrugged. 'I went back there once and found her with a younger bloke.'

'Couldn't very well have been older.'

'You have to get 'em in, don't you?' he cried, a bit like the old Stanley, I was pleased to note. I wondered what Dorelia would say if she knew her Daddy had been sleeping rough.

'Look . . .' he said, and the conversation died.

And then it was the Celtic blood stepped in again, providing me with inspiration so I knew just what to do next. I got up to go. I stood up as if many calls on my time, places to go, people to see. Been nice chatting to you, Stanley, but I have to dash.

'Look, 'Reen!' he said urgently.

'Well?' I turned my head round and looked back at him sitting there so sad and sorry for himself.

''Reeny, I ain't much . . .'

'We know.'

'But I'm . . . clean. So far's I know. I always wore . . . one of those things, you know.'

God, that must have cost him. I stared down and thoroughly enjoyed the little bastard squirming.

'You're never asking me to take you back?'

He fiddled with his cloth thread, not even looking up.

'You got a nerve.'

He nodded. 'I knew it was too much to ask,' he said. 'I gone too far. But don't forget, 'Reeny, I paid them bills. Well, I offered.'

'One half-yearly water rate, one British Telecom demand?'

'Well, it was red. And it was high, too! Blimey, sixty quid and you there all on your own!'

'It was because I was there all on my own . . .'

'Oh alright. But you got me cheques?'

'And cashed 'em.' God I was tired. I could see he was tired too.

'Moggy, please let me come home with you tonight,' he said. 'Just tonight. In the morning you can kick me out, I know I deserve it. Just tonight, though, please.'

'And why should I do that?' I asked. 'You gimme one good reason!'

'I need to check me lettuces alright.'

You can't get rooms round here unless you're a one-legged, vegetarion, black feminist, single-parent mother, and even then you got to have more than one kid by different ethnic fathers.

I took him home.

'New neighbours,' he roused himself to comment as we were standing on the step. He was looking at the beaten-up Scarecrow Ford.

'Yes,' I told him, shuddering and when we were in the hall, told him about the lilac tree.

'They can't do that!'

'They done it. And I think it was their kids who sprayed the cara.'

'Sprayed . . .? *Globe-trotter*? With cans?'

'And knocked the top off one of the gnomes' hats.'

'Oh charming!' he said. 'Bloody hell. This is turning into a right little low-class neighbourhood round here. That's not why we come 'ere when we had a bit of money.'

'Quite.' I told him about the rock music. 'It's only stopped for a bit because one of them up and died,' I said.

But I didn't tell about Claire Rayner and the settee cushions.

I done double egg and chips, all I had in the house, and then he did what he'd been dying to do all along – he went out to look at his lettuces.

I don't suppose there'll be much discussion about whether he stays but if he tries anything apart from clipping the front hedge he'll get thick ear. Might even do the settee cushions on him.

That should stop him pretty toot damn sweet.

'What about me trains?' he said at breakfast. 'You been up there?' – meaning of course, the loft, where he got model layout.

'No I haven't,' I said. I was busy poaching eggs. Didn't suppose she ever give him breakfast.

He stood in the kitchen doorway, silver stubble growth on chin, trousers and pyjama top unbuttoned. Even from where I was I could see the top hairs on his chest were turning grey. Funny, he used to be dark all over. Still at least he was wearing his pyjamas. Time was when he'd thought underwear enough.

'Better go up and check if they need watering,' I said, cutting bread for toast.

'Eh?'

'Oh, never mind. You want two bits or three?'

I didn't like the reference to trains. Brought the immediate past too much to mind. Wondered what he thought he was going to do for pieces of model railway now. There'd been one spare bit too many when bloody Sharon slag worked down at SteamPast.

But curiosity got the better of me as it usually does. I meant to be cautious and all delicate but it all come out as always.

'Where you going to get your train bits now?'

'SteamPast,' he said calmly, mouth full of toast. 'Elmer's End. There's nowhere else so good.' And he bit into piece of egg so the yellow spurted. That's men all over, innit?

'She don't go back there much, then?'

'Shouldn't think so. Still on the checkout, DIY at Demiplan.'

Oh, thanks a million. That really done me good. Just what I needed to know so early in the day — that sleaze still working for my husband's firm.

I made large pot of tea and brooded, and forgot his sugar.

Day of Bonzo's funeral. Funny, I never did find out his proper name. I didn't send no wreath, didn't even pull the front room blinds.

I would have been 'ipocryte if I did.

Went up The Feathers this evening, just the two of us. The 'Orrible Black Brian in there, going smirk, smirk, smirk.

'Good evening, Mrs Spink, and how is your lovely daughter?'

'Above your touch, anyway,' I retorted and saw him blink. Chalk one to Spinks, for once. Thank God she threw him over.

We didn't stay.

Went to The Black Swan (Mucky Duck) and Dora, her that wasn't going to serve him, said all false and smiling, 'How nice to see you both, it's been an age.'

Silly great fat cow.

Always copying me, that one. I go on a diet, she does, I try Hint-of-a-Tint (Flaming Auburn) she has to. Wonder if she following current trend in husbands?

Found that him and me could talk alright on our own except for certain words bristling all over like minefields. 'Trains' is one minefield word and 'bimbo' is another, also 'long legs', 'frizzy hair', 'pointy nose', and 'whore'.

Went home and we was talking amiable as them Regency novels say. I turned up the Magicoal because chilly and he opened two little bottles of brown ale he'd brought back from pub.

'Want some?' he asked and I jumped because I thought he suddenly prepositioning me in own unsubtle way.

Then I thought Silly! Even he wouldn't be as ridiculously fresh as all that. And I went out into the kitchen to make Ovaltine because I didn't fancy the brown ale.

He come out after me and as I was reaching up to get tin off shelf, I felt his arms go round me. I squeaked. Then I stiffened in apprehension, pretty much like Evelina with the Duke.

''Reeny, we both know I'm back for good,' he said, squeezing my new waist.

'I know nothing of the sort!' I replied tartly, clutching the Ovaltine tin.

'I swear it'll never happen again. 'Reeny,' he went on, laying his head on my chest, 'you got little tits. You need fattening up.'

'It's being so happy makes me forget to eat,' I told him all sarcastic. Well, I did eat when he was away but I can't remember what or when. Days when I used to cram Mars Bars into my mouth, holding both hands in front so bits wouldn't fall out, over long long time ago.

''Reeny, I've missed you,' he said, squeezing, bloody nerve. I knew what he was leading up to.

'No!' I yelled at him, turning round to face him.

48

'What you think I am, another of your flaming tarts, you little crumb? How *dare* you, Stanley Spink?'

'Whoops! Sorry,' he said, letting go.

'Don't you touch me!' I shouted, then lowered voice. In new-found quiet next door, they probably enjoying this.

'You can forget it,' I told him, quieter. 'I know where your thing's been, remember?'

'I told you I was clean,' he muttered.

'Clean or dirty, makes no difference to me. Keep it in your trousers.'

''Reen!'

'No.'

I mixed the Ovaltine with some hot water and poured in milk, and he came padding back after me into the lounge again.

'What, never?' he cried.

'I don't know. Probably.'

'But what am I going to *do*?'

'The usual. Who the hell cares?'

'I really blown it, then?'

''Course you bloody blown it, starting up like that. You can't just waltz in here and expect it again. It ain't natural. What do you think I am, fucking Room Service?'

He stood a bit abashed. Then he laughed hopefully. 'You could make a bit of a joke out of what you just said.'

'Don't even think about it,' I told him.

'Oh well!' he said. 'Perhaps I'll have a sherry.'

'Perhaps you won't.'

'You drunk it, then?'

'Me and the Friends. They come in day that they move out. And you're animal, that's what. Men always do it back to front. Sex, sex, sex and more sex, then if you're lucky, bit of love. Them

Hollywood novels got it wrong. Women want love first. For most women there's no such thing as instant.'

'I don't know what you're on about.'

'Well you wouldn't, would you? You think women are all homogamous commodities like slices in pre-packed bread.'

'You get the crusty bits,' he said. 'And by the way, I think you mean homogenized.'

'I know what I mean!' I said in fury.

'Keep your hair on! We got any malt whisky left still?'

Well, there was half a bottle Roderick give me for emergencies, but I'd been saving that.

'Little bit,' I said.

He brightened. Then he seemed to change his mind. He leaned forward and patted me on the arm.

'Never mind. We'll hang on to that. We'll save it for when we really got something to celebrate, eh, eh?'

Men. That Evelina should thank me I never give the Duke his balls.

I know that he's not playing around any more. How do I know? Well, for a start he rings me in his lunch hour (his idea), then he gets in prompt at half past five, often with bunch of flowers. So he picks them from the Countess' old front garden? It's just that having lived there as a child, he thinks he owns that council house down Ladywell.

I'm trying to be nice. I realize if he's back permanent, which is what I thought I wanted, I got to stop myself from shouting at him.

Difficult. And noway is he coming in my bed. Finding it hard to let him even touch me.

He does things round the house and garden and

I'm glad. Been a nuisance trying to cope alone; that front hedge got more waves in it than the Atlantic Ocean. And I'm glad neighbours can see him and know he's here and not detained somewhere, awaiting Her Majesty's Pleasure.

But do I really want him for himself?

Scarecrows quieter these days. I even seen little boy holding a blu balloon in garden that someone give him. Maybe Bonzo's death made her nicer or maybe sight of man (yes, Stanley) about the place made them all a bit more respectful. She still don't speak in street, though, and Skinny still got his gang of hustlers. I saw our Stanley looking at their thighs while operating Black 'n' Decker. I think they shouted summing at him, but of course he couldn't hear.

Been up the Duck a few times, Amy and Roderick come too. Dora impertinent, I think.

'You been ill, Stanley?'

''Reen's lost a lot of weight, hasn't she?'

And worse: 'It is nice seeing you two together. I think everyone needs someone their own age.'

After three lots of this he say going to The Feathers and I say forget that and noway and we fall out. He doesn't crack his old jokes half as much as used (you see, *some* good come out of this) and he don't laugh so loud.

And I ought to be truly grateful instead of flippant and I'm not. Everything's blimming changed. I'm miserable. And I thought I'd be so happy if I got him back.

When he come in last night I asked him if he'd seen her, couldn't stop meself.

''Course I seen her. She didn't pay me no attention.'

51

'Playing hard to get, was she?'

''Reeny, I told you.'

'Lies.'

'Godalmighty, how many more times? I don't want her!'

'– What, then?'

'I dunno.'

What he wants is summing to do with lettuces, I think. I can't give you anything but lettuce, baby . . .

And then just when I despairing – always the way – things got worse. The noise started up again next door.

I was briefly – very briefly glad, because now he'd know what I'd been on about. Half past eleven at night and that began coming through the wall. Fatgirl shot upstairs and under bed. And he got out of bed in the spare room and come in too and stood there listening. I could see he didn't believe it.

I was sitting up in bed. He walked over and thumped on the side wall, not a blind bit of good, of course, they couldn't possibly have heard. I wondered how little boy was managing to sleep through all this. Maybe he was clutching his blu balloon for comfort. Maybe Mummy and Dad Scarecrow out.

He fumed. 'I'll give 'em five minutes more,' he said. 'And then I'm going round there to complain.'

I just sat reading Woman's Own in bed. Didn't say I thought no use in going round. He would find out for himself in time.

'That's it!' he said when – oh, surprise – the noise just didn't stop. He stumped down the stairs and I heard the front door open and then – nothing. Everything continued as before. And after a bit he come back up again.

'Didn't get no answer,' he told me.

Well, well, well.

After a bit he tried again but he didn't get no answer that time either. I come downstairs and sat on the settee. Opened the August copy of *She*.

'Wish now I'd been nicer to the Passionate Friends,' I said. He stared. 'What's that got to do with it?' He lit his pipe.

Midnight come.

He went to have one more try and this time I went with him in my dressing gown for backup. Their door was plate glass like our own, that naked, fluted stuff, original 'Sixties, very dull. We got a grill on ours, wrought-iron scroll work, barley-sugar twists and twirls with *Semper Idem* in black bendy letters, tasteful.

He rang the bell and even leaned on it continual but all there was was vertebration of the music from inside. Music, I say – it was really just one long, punctuated roar.

N.B.G. I could of told him, but he weren't in mood to listen now, just getting ratty. He banged on the glass urgently with the flat of his hand and as still no answer, banged again harder and then harder still and of course that done it. Hand went through the glass.

Noise of breaking glass louder than anything I know. Star cracks appeared spreading in slow motion, then black hole come and jagged splinters slowly rising up and pointing at his arm which after a second started going drip, drip, drip.

'Oh my God!' I screamed. 'You've broken it!'

Flying, heavy footsteps now inside and startled faces all sudden in the black hole. Lights going on in the Close behind us, then old man Scarecrow peering out astonished and her with the thin lips with him, and then Skinny.

53

'Here – what you doing to my door?' Dad Scarecrow cried.

'I broke it,' Stanley said. 'I didn't mean to. I'll pay for it. I was knocking.'

'Knocking? Why knocking at this time of night?'

'We never heard you,' Skinny put in.

'I come to complain about the noise.'

'*Noise*?' thundered Dad Scarecrow. 'You come round here, breaking my bloody door because of a *noise*? *Look* at it!' he went on in injured, self-righteous indignation.

I saw Stanley sway. He doesn't often, only after gin once at a posh party.

'Look at my door!' the old man went on, as Stanley swayed. 'I mean, *look* at it! What you going to do about it? You going to pay for it or what? Look at it!'

And then there was a noise of police patrol cars in the close and the Old Bill arrived to try and sort things out.

Stan got carted off to Casuality, which left me to chat to the Police, although they did the Scarecrows first, going in next door and of course getting all wrong account – how we'd made their lives a misery with loud rows and shouting do's and things.

Then the cops come in with me and asked if Stanley violent.

I was praying none of them would be the one I kicked last New Year's Eve. We'd been dancing round the old water trough up Glenda Jackson (Ave.) and S. got mixed up with some yobs and was about to be arrested only me and Roderick came up and I kicked this cop's knees from behind so he buckled and fell over, trick I used to practise to perfection in School Assemblies, one reason why I top of list of Expulsions Pending.

54

Still they were quite nice, really and said as Stanley made offer for amount of new door, well, the glass, no charges to be made or anything. And I thought, Oh, they know Scarecrows telling big fat porky pies alright enough.

He come back about one, arm bandaged in a little sling and said he thought he'd take tomorrow off. Well, it was today already.

Spent most of what left of night listening to tap, tap of hammer on tacks in hardboard as Pop Scarecrow nailed up his front door.

It was a good sound, though not as drastic as that funeral.

Sitting on settee next morning feeling down. That business with the Scarecrows fazed me more'n it should.

'Wassup, Mog?' he said. 'Specially, I mean.'

'Place just isn't the same.'

'No, well. We'll work something out.'

'What?'

'I got idea,' he said, just as he used to do when we were courting and no place to snog.

'Have you, Stanley?'

'Trust me,' he said and made a cup of tea. Later we went up the shops and he bought me little bunch of freesias. I did liver and onions, plum crumble and ice cream for tea. Alright.

Later I was in bed, still down and shivering. Feet cold and it July and all. Maybe I in for one of my chills. Got out of bed thinking maybe have 'ot bath to warm up and there he was on the landing, holding filled stone pig, the one we bought on holiday last year. You fill it with hot water.

'For you,' he said, holding it out.

'Ta!' I said, surprised.

'You'll be alright. Take aspirin?'

'No.'

'You should.'

'Yeah.'

'Never did get round to buying that electric blanket.'

'No.'

Pause.

'You coming in, then?' I asked him.

Another pause.

'Thought I wasn't allowed.'

I said nothing.

'Be two ticks,' he said.

I went in the bedroom, pushed the pig down in the bed and put my feet on it. He wasn't allowed in, but right now I felt like child been smacked by its mother, then runs to her for comfort. He was all I had.

He come in all careful because of his arm and we just lay there, an old pair of crocks, he said. I thought maybe I been saving up for this for days, what with the Scarecrow aggro and everything. I was cold, I was hot. I tossed and turned all night.

In the morning he brought me up dark toast, hardboiled egg and no salt on a tray for breakfast and I cried.

Tea he'd made was alright though, and that what mattered. I drank five cups and sent him down for more. By Saturday evening I was fine again and strong.

And just as well.

'Only one thing for it,' he said Sunday morning. 'Gotta move.'

'Sell the house, you mean?'

'Won't be able to buy a better one if we don't.'

He folded his *News and Screws* in half and then in quarters, the way he does when thinking, and I looked at him. We were in the lounge at the time. And he'd hardly glanced at *TV star in hotel arrest with willing nymph as fans invade.*

'A *better* one?' I said.

'Don't want a worse one, do you?'

'I never thought of moving. Not really.'

'No?' he said, jerking his head towards next door.

They'd had a party there last night, well, someone had. I got a feeling that all done on purpose; Ma and Pa went out — God knows what happened to the baby — and Skinny had his mates in of both sexes. There was probably summing else going on as well but you certainly couldn't hear it above the din.

Police come when we called them, twelve o'clock, but prompt at half past twelve the racket soared again.

And when I looked at the garden this morning I found we was clean out of gnomes. They'd all been smashed except the one with the already broken hat. (I found him under the caravan, much later.)

He saying now we should get new house, call it by same name, *Semper Idem*, have everything the way we always had it, get new gnomes . . .

'Calling it *Semper Idem* put the mockers on it in the first place,' I said bitterly. 'No, I wouldn't want that.'

'We just got to start again, though.'

'Yes. Everything's bloody changed.'

'Well brace yourself for summing else,' he said, opening paper again, after looking at thigh pic without hardly thinking. 'DemiPlan's offering early retirement for selected personel, the over hem-hems, and I'm toying with the idea of taking it.'

'Get away,' I said, sitting up.

'There's a pension,' he said. 'But don't get too excited – it would mean a cut in income by about two thirds. *But* . . .' he went on, rustling *Screws* and leaning forward, 'if we play everything alright, I think we'd manage.'

'Manage?' I said suspiciously. 'What's this *manage*?' Because I still wanted that electric blanket. And a dishwasher. And loada new clothes, Littlewoods M.O. How everything come down to money in the end! *Dosh.* What you can provide.

'Well I meant a bit more than manage, naturally,' he said a bit testy. 'But what we do. We sell the house and buy a cheaper one and invest the profit. That pays a monthly interest, follow me? So you got second income to top up the pension.'

'You said *better* house just now. We don't want no two up, two down sort of thing with a tin bath in the back yard.'

'Good enough for my Mum – and for yours.'

'Not the point, is it? We come a long way since.'

And that is true. Middle class, us, now. *Petit bourgeois.* I know because Wayne told me.

'Right. It don't have to be no titchy place. House prices being what they are, in this neck of the woods we're sitting on a gold mine. We sell this, we got enough to buy a really posh and pretty place – four bedrooms, proper dining room, large gardens, back and front.'

'Trout stream?' I asked him sarcastic.

'Maybe, if you want one. All depends. Think, Moggy – a historic setting for all our little bits! How about real beams, ingle nook and all?'

'Go on.'

'Trufe,' he said, striking a fresh match and lighting pipe.

58

'*In London?*' He wasn't sane.

'Ah. There, now you got it. Clever girl. No, not exactly in London. Not exactly. Still I think we've had enough of London, haven't we? We want to get away from London.'

'I don't,' I told him.

He look at me and just went on smoking his pipe. He knows when to stop.

'Alright, alright,' he said, shaking out *News and Screws*. 'You don't want to know about my lovely plan, forget it. Forget I spoke. Forget about real beams and ingle nooks and all.' And he puffed away.

I went to peel potatoes in the kitchen but idea of ingle nook intrigued me. I did the beans and mix a Yorkshire and fed the Yorkshire puddy tat before I'd even noticed.

Is ingle nook the place you go for ingle bitty nooky?

We had dinner and he didn't say much. Fell asleep in armchair and I let him. I was thinking of horse brasses, wasn't I and copper warming pans, four poster beds, them antique globe things on a stand you use for drinks . . .

Quietly I got the M.O. catalogue to see what lovely things on offer and found a triffic mahogany-colour, solid wood, four-tier, period whatnot with matching telephone table and seat covered in hard-wearing Dralon, also directory box and useful under-shelf. When he woke up again, I all excited, though naturally I didn't let him see.

Made a pot of tea. He saw the catalogue, which I hadn't had time to shut, and his eyeballs sort of flickered. But not a word between us further – well, he watching old Sophia Loren film (I mean old *film*) and breathing quite a bit, especially when her frock

59

got wet and gulping down digestives. Well Sunday always a day for good old tits and bums, as well as food.

I got the tea. I done curried eggs in salad, cold marinaded turkey we had left from in the week, salami, baked potatoes, cold apple tart and cream. Then we had another pot of tea and finished up some of that garlic cheese with hi-baked water biscuits and some butter.

'That's better!' he cried, pushing his plate away and lolling back. You'd think I never fed him in the week. 'You been looking at all new furniture, then?' He knew damn well I had. 'Have to get all new if we follow my plan.'

I'd been wondering how soon we'd get back to that.

'So where is this dream house?' I asked, not serious. And then, right there as he opened his mouth to reply, I knew what he was going to say before he said it.

'*Norfolk*,' he said. 'We move there or somewhere, we got London money to burn.'

'Yeah?'

'Yeah. Would I lie?' He hurried over that one because we both knew that he has been known to, and he fished out dirty old page torn from some local Norfolk newspaper and spread it in between the plates. I cleared. When I come back he'd got our own local paper too, open at property pages.

'Look at these for prices!' he said, pounding on the table with the first finger of a hand. 'Look at these and then tell me if I'm right or not!'

'Oh I dare say you're right alright,' I said. 'Question is, do we want to go?'

'One of us does,' he growled.

'It's too far.'

'Only 150 miles, nothing to modern cars.'

'And we'd really have pot of money over?'

'On my oath. You do 'rithmetic.'

I didn't need to. I can take £40,000 from £80,000 without pencil and paper and our generation weren't brought up to use a calc. Well they hadn't thought of them then. I stood thinking.

'Forty thousand quid . . .' I said. 'And we still got them Telecom shares, and there's my Consolidated British Foods.'

'I got you, in't I?' he said, lighting pipe.

'Not you, and don't you think it.' I went to make another pot of tea. This time when I come back he had the catalogue.

'Look at this!' he said. 'Would you Adam and Eve it?' He began to read. '*Matching, budget-priced, brass-finished, acid-etched bola glass* – that's a light fitting, 'Reen – *threelight flush.* There's a bit of tasteful old antiquity for you. Or how about this? *Rise 'n' fall swing-thing in "Swirl" collection, elegantly decorated glass panels allied with quality brassed metal work* . . .'

'Just drink your tea,' I said.

Didn't tell him I already set me heart on 'Bouquet', *threelight pendant on chain suspension with thirty delicate glass flowers, clear or pink,* £59.99. I was saving that until I see how much money we got left in kitty after . . .

After . . .

After the sale.

After the sale of *Semper Idem.*

We had this man come from the Estate Agents to give us valuation of the house. He went all round looking at things and measuring with a steel rule. Still, I'd hoovered pretty thoroughly, oh yes.

61

He wouldn't give us verbal, not even when S. pressed him, but letter come next day.

'Bloody stroll on!' he said, though he must of been expecting it. 'Six or seven times what we paid for it!'

I was chuffed, we both were. And then of course the would-be buyers started coming – we had told the Agents that they could – and after that there weren't no more peace for . . .

. . . twenty-four hours. We sold *Semper Idem* first go off, very next morning. Well it was in good nick and front hedge cut and Skinny Scarecrow out.

'Stanley,' I said, speaking all level because really worried. 'We sold up, well agreed to sell, and got no place to go I hope you know.'

'All in hand, duck,' he said. 'I been to see about retirement.'

'How does that get us a house?'

'I took a fortnight's holiday in lieu of September pay and I got annual three weeks owing. You get busy with addresses from *The Lady* like you did last time – you always say you get a better class of oik in there – and we'll go up to Norfolk.'

'How about Sandringham?' I asked. 'Good class of oik at Sandringham.'

'Just *do* it,' Stanley said. 'There's sure to be somewhere left.'

And he was right.

Sold *Globe-trotter* today. Got £1,500. Found hatless gnome underneath and brought him indoors. S. said he would make new hat for him out of modelling clay.

Put ad in *Cars for Sale* column local paper. I'm

not going in it after *she's* been sitting there and told him so.

Went up the timberyard and bought five new gnomes with fishing rods and red pointy caps. Keeping them indoors.

Letters arriving from solicitor, name of Caroline, after the Radio, I presume. Said to him (he got her), 'Trust you to pick a girl.'

Still, she seems to know her stuff.

Dear Mr and Mrs Spink,

Re the proposed sale of No. 1, Kitchener Close . . .

He all excited now, hankering (I can see) after his putrative roots in Norfolk and hoping noble family will come to call. Still hoping his father is the nice old boy who turned up at his mother's funeral, one who told us he loved Countess when she 'ousemaid at Burlingham Hall.

Wayne too all wistful. Says he has a good mind to chuck teaching and write poetry instead. I said rather sharp, 'What about the baby?' And he said she couldn't write much yet but no doubt would' when she was older.

Looked at him with good hard stare like Paddington.

This American (buyer) come round, bringing his wife and children to see house. They said they was Anglophiles, which I always thought was stamps.

He full of admiration for the English Public School and said that in the Land of the Free they were called private schools. I said they were here, too. Stanley said, 'Land of the free what?'

Told the Poor Colonial I sorry about Stanley and I'd take him away. And this Yankee – he was from

South Carolina – smiled sweetly as if heard joke before.

Lovely manners. Especially gone on my knee-height toning dildo on kitchen wall. He seemed amused by it when I explained it seen a lot of service – but not half so amused as Stanley when this American said he'd just get his windbreaker when he going home because wind chilly.

Sometimes I'm dead embarrassed by that Stanley; if he got noble blood then I'm a monkey. And he will snigger so and say if only I had seen him doing National Service . . . On Gumment orders they put bromide in the tea, he says, to stop unmentionables happening.

I really don't think we wish to know that now, do we?

Not quite nice.

We got Lancia, FIRE LX with total power output 45 bhp at 5,000 rpm, front electric window, central door lock, split folding rear seats, internally adjustable driver, door mirrors, rear window wash/wipe, overhead camshaft fully integrated robotized engine with turbo charger and intercooler.

Also ducky little red go-faster stripe down side.

'Nice car,' I told him. 'Like it.'

Renting little new semi-bungalow on edge of Sheringham, pretty town on coast but full of crabs (all sorts).

Den of antiquity. So slow to cross the road. And these skeletons never signal when they're driving. Even the knuckle-walking Bonzo was livelier than these. Still maybe some on 'oliday, taking things easy. Charity. But he nearly driven out to lunch by driving.

'Just think, some of these descendants of those who had awayday rape and pillage tickets long ago,' he said, gazing round. (We were in pub.) 'This is all inbreeding and scrumpy drinking, if you ask me.'

'The young ones are alright.'

'Yes, but the old . . .'

'Look on the bright side, why don't you,' I told him. 'At least they won't be into heavy metal rock.'

We had settled into a three—four houses a day routine and hadn't liked any of them so far. He moaned about the price of food in pubs. And he told me to stop showing off.

'You gotta merge,' he said. 'Be quiet. You can't just come up here and walk all over.'

'Merge my backside,' I said. 'These provincials lucky to be getting Purkiss blood at all.'

No luck at all until second week. Then we found this little village, Dodderham, about describes it. Anything less like London hard to imagine. One little bendy lane called The Street, gloomy pub, Red Lion, and a small general store/Post Office, sold wellies, a really jumping sort of place. My heart sank. I all set to hightail it out of Dodderham.

And then I saw the building at the end.

It was still going on, some of it, there was scaffolding up. And it was all in local cobblestone and flints; they stuck out from the walls like little bums.

All the new building was round a granite sett courtyard called The Square and there were pots of geraniums outside the finished ones. They had stained woodwork and little window boxes too. I never see anything so pretty.

Used to think Kitchener Close was nice, but it was nothing to The Square. And no litter either, no lager cans, no fag packs, no ice cream cones or used-up condoms. It even had a distant glimpse of the sea through what passes for hills up here, like summing out of picture book.

And it was not far from Nat Truss place where Countess first a 'ousemaid long ago. Nine months longer than he is old, to be exact.

Oh, he wanted to come here. But I could see him being cunning with great flat heavy feet. We sat in The Red Lion and he said he didn't think Dodderham suitable place *at all*.

'What?' I said. 'Not Eve's Patch?' For that was the name of a little pink-painted house we'd seen about eleven, up for sale next to the general stores. There weren't nothing left for sale in The Square.

Eve's Patch had trees all round, nice flowering ones like laburnam and Japanese cherry. It had a secretive front garden, flagstones in winding path, vegetable patch to the side and long, long stretch at the back ending in a wild bit with some pine trees. There was nothing after the pine trees, just open fields. And inside, the rooms had real oak beams and there was ingle nook with little side seats, ever so quaint and nice.

It also had three bedrooms, was detached and half the price of *Semper Idem*. Agent told us if we come two years previous, could have had it for a song.

'Course he'd seen me looking at it, liking it, and now determined to make me really sure. Nearly overplayed his hand though, silly prat, because said summing about staying in South Norwood after all. I just said right, let's go then, Scarecrows'll be glad to see us back and give us rock band welcome maybe. And he cleared his throat and thought we just have one more look round while we here.

The owner was a Mrs Dorling, absentee landlord letting as 'oliday cottage, though everything very clean. S. went and borrowed the pub phone.

'No chains!' I heard him telling the Estate Agent. 'We don't want no selling chains. We know all about those and we don't want one, thank you very much.'

Well we didn't. We bin on one with *Semper Idem*; one person falls out of line, all do, domino effect.

We was assured no chains, just honest one-to-one sale, and we made our offer, which was asking price and it accepted over phone. We went back and looked at house – then realized we got three days buckshee. I got quite brown on beach.

Oh, we had rows; he happened to worry out loud about getting lettuces in up here at precisely same time I cutting bread and I jagged my thumb and said summing to him very crisp. Still, it muted stuff mostly. We got on well.

And that Caroline kept the letters coming! He said give her great big bunch of flowers when all wound up, she so efficient. Didn't realize we'd have to pay for all her keeping tabs on us. But that come later.

Home.

And almost immediately into trouble, because that's the way, in't it, you don't hardly let yourself feel happy; some great hand gonna come down out of sky and say, 'Take that, you little runt!'

Darling Mrs Dorling had decided to sell Eve's Patch after all to someone else.

Stan told Caroline straight. 'We're being gazumped?' he said on phone. 'She holding us to ransom – or what? Find out.'

Caroline rang back to say Mrs D. hoping for more.

'That's it, then,' Stanley said. 'Forget it. Wash it out and tell her to get stuffed.'

I never admired our Stanley more, even though it was she who was stuffing us. All the same, though, very down. American pressing on our sale. I wanted Eve's Patch very much, the more when I couldn't have her.

Up a tree.

And then maybe gazumper fell under bus or summing (no, I didn't use the settee cushions) for that Dorling changed her mind again and Caroline told us we got lot, curtains, fitted carpets and all if we still wanted. Vendor eager exchange contracts soon as possible.

Over moon. Getting tea chests, sugar boxes, cardboard cartons, newspaper and beginning packing up. Who would imagine you collect so much in fifteen years? Junk, I mean. S. making many little trips to tip in Lancia with plastic sacks.

Wayne still behaving as if death immanent and grouchy.

I said, 'It's not that far. You were the one who told me Aussies and Canadians go that far just for an evening's partying.'

He said, 'All that loneliness! The woods and fields and coast that goes on for miles. I could really write poetry up there.'

Didn't know what to say except I hoped it wouldn't be as lonely as all that. Still at least this time we taking gnomes with us. Stanley has mended Redcap and I made him fishing rod to match the rest.

And now we got Financial Adviser, really nice man came to lunch just like TV commercial with bunch of roses for me from own garden.

I did Sole, because he middle class, and Chocolate Bomb, and Stanley said, 'What's this thing? Shit Surprise?'

Nearly hit him.

Prayed Scarecrow noise wouldn't start up while we having drinks on patio and just for once it didn't. Think they was all out.

F.A. stayed about three hours, partaking of dry white wine and smiling a good deal. Felt confident that he would handle money most securely.

Then – off down the High Street (me) flashing the Bard Card right and left and getting things for Norfolk; two olive-green Barbours, his 'n' hers, lotsa polo necks in tasteful colours, green wellies with little buckles to them, a leather flying jacket for him with two-way pockets and a fly-front zip fastening.

He wouldn't wear the wellies and he said the flying jacket affectation. So hurt by this I had to turn away to hide the tears and he asked what up.

I said I thought he should be *glad* I so in with his schemes to go all countrified and he said yes, but not poncey County set and I said what about noble relatives then and that halted him. He tried the wellies on for size.

Things all too busy and exciting now. Think I shall leave Diary for a while, hide it somewhere he can't see and read. Hot drawer of the gas oven a good place. I mean, he never cooks. I mean.

God, what a nightmare. Fatgirl in back of 'atchback, crying even though doped for the journey by vet, all among extra last-minute stuff piled in by me, which made him cross.

Me crying because leaving *Semper Idem.*

He putting up with it all along London Orbital then saying distracted, 'Why the *fuck* can't you stop blubbing?'

I said, 'You forgot my birthday this year.'

He said, 'Your birthday. Fifth May. Oh my God.' He remembering he with slag Lollipop at the time. That shut him up and I was able to grizzle in peace.

Stopped at Dartford Tunnel though because I saw Dorelia ahead in the Fiat; she cut her Daddy up on purpose and made him swear. Had what looked like Baby Jane asleep in back. She'd never said a dicky-bird about coming to help us move.

'Follow that car!' I told him, and Fatgirl let out a yell as if disagreeing.

They say the mind blocks out what it don't care to remember. I think this true. Beyond the sight of the removal van ahead, hurtling and swaying into village, I can't remember much.

Do know there were garden things in living room, garage things in garden shed. And still he tipped the buggers! Said anything to get rid of them.

Writing now surrounded by boxes, boxes, boxes. Poor Fatgirl staggering about with eyeballs rolling wildly in her head.

D. and little Janie stayed the night. I worried about baby but she slept fine and left this afternoon, taking her mother with her.

Now we got business of putting things away.

Nightmare feeling wearing off a bit. Hot weather, but everything very green. Cat recovered, thinks she must have died and gone to heaven. This morning four voles, two big mice and a little mouse all laid out in neat row by the freezer. He thought that was sweet, said she wanted them frozen for when there weren't none. I told him silly and sentimental.

He said proudly, 'Hunting cat after all, you see.' I said, 'Don't kid yourself. She don't stalk and chase and leap – just rolls on prey. Nothing don't stand a chance under that great weight.' He said, 'You don't like her, do you, I can tell.'

I do like her, but she just ain't Plum. I know she's Plum's daughter but she just ain't Plum and that's that.

He said, 'Blimey, not going to blub again, are you?'

He don't understand a thing can't be a substitute for something, you got to like it for itself alone.

We got pond here, bigger than *Semper Idem* [sic], so I put new gnomes round edge and gave the best place to the mended one. He painted sign for gate saying Eve's Patch, a bit wobbly but plenty of curls and flourishes on the letters, and I hung up wire basket by front door with fuschia cuttings that our Amy gave me.

Very quiet and dark here, nights. Can't get used to having no street lights, and said so to Stan. He confessed he similarly disturbed.

So we went down into the town and bought some coloured bulbs, the sort you put in outside trees at Christmas and strung them round the porch. It takes away effect of total dark at night and you don't notice stars and moon so much. I mean, they very obvious out here and sort of staring down. They gimme willies.

He said maybe we get floodlights for the garden later, eh? And I said, 'Ooh yes, and fancy carriage lanterns for the garridge.'

'Real Stately 'ome,' he said. We laughed. I thought of giving guided tours even, and talking in ladida voice. Made him smile.

After that we bought swing lounge settee for the back, all done ever so tastefully in Jacobean tapestry, and a round white table, looks like metal

71

really with brilliant floral pub-type umbrella and white curly chairs to match like that poor French queen had. Also a gas bottle barbie on wheels and a portable white plastic drinks caddy with holes for the bottles and glasses. Also two bright pink lilo's and a reclining padded armchair with footrest in Jacobean to match the swing, three folding tubular steel chairs with day-glo covering, a paddleball set and a real string hammock to go under the far trees. I wanted clock golf, croquet and a yoghurt maker for the lawn but he said OTT, not made of bleedin' money.

Then time to do indoors, all cottagey. He painting window frames and wooden pelmets pink, me sewing curtains up in lovely material with big roses on, not like fainthearted Regency stripe she had before, also chintzy covers with deep, deep frills for the furniture. I want roses everywhere, the bigger the better.

I got big wickerwork baskets with enormous fancywork handles hanging from kitchen beam, I got that from middle pages of *Good Housekeeping*, also bunches of herbs dangling to dry. Not quite sure what they are, though. Me Willow Pattern on kitchen dresser and big barometer on the wall you tap. Also oil lamps all around, we're really tradish, almost Nineteenth Century in Eve's Patch; he busy fixing leads to lamps and wiring up three-pin plugs.

Spare moments, we go down to town to junk shop and buy horse brasses, copper jug, a warming pan or three, five toasting forks, brass coal scuttle (repro, but you can't tell), ancient ship's clock and ships's wheel for the wall, large brass, free-standing elephant and greyhound, fancy fire dogs and log basket with 'andles to it, very rustic.

The Magicoal looks very poor and small in 'earth.

I think we'll have to get a bigger, though he said don't be daft, we'll get real logs and have a proper fire.

I don't know. All that ash. Still perhaps if I line log basket with plastic swing bin liner it won't be so bad, at least that will keep a check on bits from logs.

We went into a neighbour's, her that has the Stores, very kindly asked us in for drinks and I see she got logs stacked up either side of 'earth all picturesque.

I got spider plants too, all about the lounge.

Now things more like home. Made a beautiful arrangement of some white stuff I found down by trees in a jug and put it in empty 'earth. He moaned it stank; I found out later it was called cow parsely!

Not quite nice.

Can't wait now for people to come up and visit. Amy will be just wild with envy. But not until I get spare bedrooms all done up with wooden (imitation) candle brackets, rose-patterned duvies for the beds (must get a couple of divans) and repro Victorian washstands with marble tops and jugs.

He out planting lettuce seed for autumn as I write, got little leanto greeenhouse against wall. Took him out a cup of tea and he said happy as pigs in shit, us now, eh, eh?

I said what about working, don't he miss it, and he said yeah, the way you do when 'eadache goes away.

'Get up when you please, wear your old clothes, no yes, sir, no, sir, three bags full. Best of all I'm doing what I enjoy.'

'Planting lettuce seed?'

'What's wrong with that?'

Well I dunno, but strikes me as a bit dull. Still, each to his own. And then I asked him slyly don't he miss the boys and girls?

'A bit,' he admitted. 'But you put that against all this! No comparison.'

Maybe. But I'm thinking it could get just a teeny bit lonely here.

Went down the town for more horse brasses, because if more is good, a whole lot more is a whole lot better, I think. And it was while we were in this great big junk shop that I learned crunch reason why he left that little tart.

She laughed at his toupée.

Found it on the floor beside the bed, laughed and said, 'Summing just crawled in 'ere to die! Step on it, quick!'

I didn't laugh, honest. Didn't say nothing — just stared straight ahead at some dead classy brass notices you could buy to put up on your walls. A bit of Brasso bring them up a treat, I thought. There was *Duck or Grouse* for low ceilings, seen that one before, *Heads* — not sure about that one — and *Little Mermaids' Room*, which I fancied for the downstairs toilet.

I wondered why he'd given up wearing the stupid thing, and now I knew. That Lollipop hurt our Stanley's pride.

'Prefer you without it anyway,' I told him casual and he said, 'Do you, Moggy?' in little voice as if quite grateful.

'Have some of those brass signs, eh?' he went on all brisk. 'Do for around the house. You choose the ones you want, I'll fix 'em up.'

So now we got *Gally* on the kitchen door, *Heads* — it means toilet — up and down. I put in a plea for

74

Little Mermaids but he said that was sexist, Little Pirates got to wee-wee too.

We got *Captain's Table* for the dining room, he ever so chuffed with that one, and me too. I never had a proper dining room before, in South Norwood you had breakfast bars and dinerettes.

Now – the postman comes ten o'clock unless he stopped off for elevenses with his Auntie, when it could be any time, depends if he stays on for dinner.

The milkman comes three days a week.

The dustman – well, I asked around and got reply 'that du vary' – only I can't do a Norfolk accent written down.

I know her in the shop now, too, name's Mavis and is a nice clean body comes from Essex. We swap diet notes because I got to watch it; temptation is to let yourself go when there's none to see. She says she's a medium.

'Yes,' he said, 'medium what?' predictable when I told him. I said 'Summing like Doris Youknow. Big girl, wears Crimpleen.' Well they all called Doris these days, wear big Crimpleen and talk to dear Departed.

Waited for him to ask, 'Departed what?' but he knew that one. Just said, 'Wonder if it's true? There's some I shouldn't half like to hear speak from the grave. Stephenson, built the Rocket, Father of British Rail, for a start. And of course there's that Isambard Kingdom Brunel.'

'Ring her up, why don't you?' I say. 'Maybe she get him for you on her weejee board.'

But it had shocked me all the same. I mean fancy giving innocent little baby name like that. No wonder he built bridges when grown up. Most likely making plans to go and jump right off.

His trains stay in their boxes on big shelf in garridge. I said nothing but I think he thinks I think he thinks forbidden now or sort of. Anyway, not popular, all past associations and so on. But that's up to him.

I'm relieved to think he's over a hundred miles away from little tart, but as for bedtime in the country . . . well, best you can say is he don't wear thermal socks no more (it's August anyway) but nice new purple pyjamas I got him with dragons on, done in my Super Electronic De Luxe at lo-temperature, using lo-rinse blu bubble thing approved by EEC and ironed beautifully using hi-finish, carnation-smelling fabric conditioner and spray starch (planet friendly). I like to get a good knifelike crease right up the legs both sides and under the arms. He moans like suit of armour.

Is that why he can't . . .? Surely not. It'll come back in time and then he'll be like he used, all pink and fortuitous and demanding.

And God alone knows how I'll feel about it then.

Up Red Lion, blasted with White Satin, wearing my Danish blu. Don't think they seen woman in trousers in here before. I prance about a bit and he says, 'Hush!'

Mavis medium from Stores inside with publican's wife. He looked at her a bit sideways as if afraid she might break out and speak with tongues, or summing, but she never.

Locals all round bar and saying things in dialect. I think they do it on purpose when we come in. One bloke in corner with his legs stuck out built like brick shit house and no messing, watching scene with face all unmoving but that's nothing, they all

76

do that round here. Not like Londoners. Solid. Still, not stupid. Thought they was at first but found out I was wrong.

This chap had grey eyes and very short blond hair, most Nordic, leather jacket on like Stan's, torn jeans, faded but very clean. He had a cloth bag down by his feet and once or twice I thought I see the bag move and travel a little way along the bare floor boards.

'Alright,' I said to Stanley, nodding my head in the direction of the jacket.

'And if you were years younger,' he said, which puzzled me for a moment.

I sat trying to merge but I forgot once and laughed out loud at something the landlord said. He dug me sharply in the ribs to make me shut up.

Well after another twenty minutes of faces all still and the occasional 'Ooh-ar!', I was beginning to get very bored, but just then the door opened and in come a crowd of young people, said they were on a treasure trail with cars. They got up the landlord's tits I could see with their 'Half of shandy and six straws, please!' and talking too loud in very middle-class voices.

Chap over in the corner with the legs was watching them all the time.

I and Stanley sat where we were, merging, and I could see locals getting fed up too. There wasn't a jukebox or nothing to drown the sound of their voices and they got louder and louder and fuller of their own concerns, mostly about whom was rogering who. They seemed to think everyone wanted to know that Jeremy's wife was having it off with Rupert and seeing Alistair behind both backs (if that's atomically possible) while Fiona was rolling about with Charles. I mean, who cares?

77

Well I did, for a start. Anything for a bit of human interest in this morgue. But as I say, the natives were getting restless.

Then suddenly there was a scream from one of the girls and she climbed a bar stool pretty toot damn sweet and all the loud talking dwindled to roar and then a hum and then went out entirely.

Then there were more screams.

'Oh I say!' one of the young men called out – and there running along the bar was this little furry yellow animal, peaky little face and tail. Scuffles broke out as the girls broke ranks and tried to get away. And then two more of the beasts came scampering happily across the floor to join their friend.

The bar emptied fast of Henriettas and their men went after them and how those locals laughed. First time I see their faces change all evening. I didn't see the animals disappear, but suddenly they was gone.

'*Callum*,' Mavis said, wiping her eyes. But when I turned to look at where the large bod had been sitting I saw he was at the door of the pub with the cloth bag over his shoulder. He winked once at the assembled company and then went out.

'Ain't you seen ferrets before now?' Mavis said.

I told her I didn't think you got them south of the River.

'You should see Callum with his lurcher,' Mavis went on. 'Delicate as a cat, she is, mostly greyhound. And jackdaws, pair of them, say things you wouldn't believe a bird could say.'

'Rude things?' our Stanley put in chuckling.

'Oh yes. And he's got cats, and chickens – good place to go for pullets if you ever want any – ducks and geese. And pheasants that he's raised from eggs.'

'What's a pheasant look like, anyway?' Stanley said. 'I fink I only ever seen them plucked and strung.'

I met Callum once or twice since then. He lives in a converted railway carriage with acre of land around right at the end of The Street. Always nods civil when he sees me, more'n you can say for some of 'em round here.

Mavis says he poaches and of course I thought she meant eggs though it was pheasants really, and how you poach whole pheasant at a time beats me.

'Whole ones?' I asked her and she said, 'Of course,' looking at me a bit oddly.

Surely you would have to chop them up? Unless there's a special pan for that sort of thing up here.

Stanley no wiser than me except he thought you'd have to pluck them first.

'Well, natch,' I said. 'Anyone can see that. What a dumbo you are, Stanley,' I said to him.

That Callum's father come in the Stores while I was chatting to Mavis about diet books this morning. She had a new one which explained parabolas, them things them naughty Olympic athletes take to boost performances.

Callum's dad looked like a Viking; lean, tanned face, blu eyes, reminded me of Edward Devereux, nobleman Stan likes to think his father.

He nodded politely but I don't think he liked seeing strangers in the village. I thought he only spoke to Mavis because she come from Essex.

And because he wanted stamps of course.

Mavis told me he the rightful owner of The Square: his ancestors had farmed the land about for generations, minor gentry in their way who used to live in fifteenth-century manor house somewhere towards Aylsham. But death duties and taxation forced him to sell land and property, with little to hand on to his son by way of inheritance.

This struck me as very sad. I went home and told Stanley. I think I shall make him hero of Romantic novel.

S. just opening post when I got in, and crumpling up an envelope in his hand.

'Didn't know she could write, your tart,' I said and he said, 'Pension Form, dummy. It's me notification come through, tells you how much tax and at what rate, the monthly amount and so on.'

He frowned, studying bit of paper.

'Not worried, are you?' I said, noticing his face.

'Tax is higher than I thought.'

'There's our investments. Don't forget our investments. We'll be rolling in it once they send the book.'

So we will. This Financial Adviser showed us how to put money in huge finance company, who then make you monthly payment via your local branch of Building Society and you can draw on them like a bank only instead of cards or a cheque book you have little blu pass book.

Only trouble was little blu pass book hadn't been issued to us yet.

When it has, like I said, we'll be rolling in it.

House all finished now. Even got telephone extension in bedroom.

Wondering what to do. I mean, place like summing out of *Homes and Gardens*. What's left to do? Got to be more to life than just going up the pub with him.

He said, 'Autumn lettuces are showing. Shallots are doing nicely too.'

Thrillsville.

He said, 'Wasser matter? You feeling homesick?'

Sort of.

He said, 'Well, we done it now. We burned our boats. We can't go back, not unless you wanna take titchy little house or we win the Pools. House prices aren't going to hit the heights up here the way they did down south.'

Oh no! I'd never thought of things like that! No going back?

'What's that poet you're always quoting at me recently? The one whose friend came to a tragic end?'

'Patience Strong?'

'Tennyson. That's it. *"Courage!" he said . . .'*

'*"Courage!" he said, and pointed towards the . . .*'

'Pub,' said my Stanley. 'He pointed towards the pub. Bloody good idea. Come on, Moggy. What you waiting for, Christmas?'

Took a picnic to a deserted part of the beach today, all stones and no EEC safe blu water flag. Still, lot of scenery; cliffs and rolling fields for miles and miles and miles.

R.S.P.B. got a lot of the land round here and filled it up with twitchers. They carry tripods for their telescopes and cameras in all weathers and get all frantic seeing avocet (bird, not intersurface missile). Stanley caused uproar by walking among them saying he fancied it for dinner, roasted with little green peas.

House in the Park nearby got pillars in the front, you could tell that it was wealthy. And there were cattle grazing all around under the big trees, just as Edward Devereux had said, only they weren't all black and white and called Daisy; these sweet pretty dusky browns and greys, long-haired and got little tits and number tags in ears, like 'Reen.

Of course nothing stopped him from having good gawp at the house. Me, I'd have been fine with the stable block, which had cobbled yard and a blu-faced clock on the tower.

There had been a lake too nearby but they filled it in on account of not being what Capability Brown had said (or says, not sure if he dead yet), he commanding, whoever he is, a lot of say-so. I know Callum pissed off about the lake because he used to fish there.

'What you think then, Moggy, eh?' he said gazing round. 'But for a twist of fate all this might have been ours.'

Bloody great big one, if you can call the Countess a twist of fate, though no doubt she slimmer then and hadn't the whiskers.

Still, she his mother after all so didn't say anything. Though judging by the way she seems to have put herself about, his father could have been *anybody*. But that too I didn't say. (Tact.)

Fees (bill) come from Caroline (solicitor) today.

I said, 'And you were going to send her a great big bunch of flowers.'

He said, 'Changed me mind, in't I? How about quick note saying "Up yours!" instead?'

We put the itemized bill on kitchen table and went through bits one by one. He said when we finish, 'Blimey, no wonder you never see a poor solicitor.'

Not made as much profit as we thought. A good chunk eaten away by Caroline's dealing with Mrs

Dorling when first she would and then she wouldn't sell. All those letters and phone calls – every one of them charged for, and payable by us. Thought of doing the settee cushions on Mrs Dorling.

Maybe I could get a job. Not much point in him trying, liable to lose pension if works for more than two days in a week. I made some enquiries, but mostly only chambermaiding available, in coast hotels and such like, during summer months, and paying *under £2 an hour.*

I told the D.H.S. I told the Job Centre.

'This wouldn't do for London!' I said quite sharp.

They wasn't very helpful in reply. I said, 'Don't you talk to me in that tone!' and hung up on them straight, the poor provincials. Still, didn't help with problem. Rather stuck.

Lot of black economy round here. That Callum always working for someone, for example, and I'm pretty sure he don't bother about no P45 or his N.I. stamp or his income tax return.

Went into Mavis'. Moaning loudly that anything under £2 an hour ridiculous in London when some locals come in shop and I got looked at a bit sideways.

Poor provincials.

Racking brains.

My educated son-in-law always smiled pleasantly when I used to say I had ambitions to become a teacher. Mind he also smiled pleasantly when reading me poetry; he's an encouraging sort of bloke. So I reckon I could do it. There's a little Nursery School mile and a half away from here on outskirts of next village I found on long lonely walk between flat fields. I often go there now we got this lovely September weather; they've got a

83

little playground surrounded by iron railings, with a huge old chestnut tree in the centre and a slatted seat running all round underneath. Term just begun again and young mothers cluster round the gate and wave to their children going in to school.

Takes me back. Like to think I might be one of them again. In a dim light I fancy I pass for thirty.

'And the rest!' he said rudely when I told him.

Uncouth prat.

Raining now on odd days so walks not always on. Into Mavis' to chat but she busy. Asked her if she ever took Wednesday off, when closed, thinking we might go into Norwich together on the bus, but she said even Sunday spent doing VAT.

'Sounds like hard graft,' I told her and she said had it up to *here*, chucking shop soon and going back to Essex she shouldn't wonder, live with her daughter, maybe char a bit, anything be less work than sodding Stores.

And I only just got to know her. Feeling sad.

Tried to chat up Callum in the street. He carrying gun.

I said, 'Oh Callum, are you going to shoot things with that weapon?' And he thought a bit and finally said no, not if they dead already when he got there.

Always sweetish, dry smell about that man, not tobacco, but something like it.

Later met him coming out of Square balancing large ladder on his shoulder. Been mending summing high, you can't fool 'Reen.

I said, 'Oh Callum, didn't see you there!' And he said not surprising really, he always near-invisible when carrying enormous ladder.

He had his beautiful grey lurcher to heel with

him. Looked as if she could run a bit an' all. She
sniffed the air around me but very shy. Still at least
he speaks when spoken to, which is more than most
do in The Street.

Evening spent polishing brass and rearranging
warming pans until he got ratty and snapped why
couldn't I relax?

I know what it is – it's all to do with how's yer
father and he won't discuss it. That side of life
entirely gone it seems. He just rolls over.

Touched him the other night, meaning just cuddle
really and he said, 'Sorry, Mog, I'm so tired!'

Tired?

I can't make him out.

He keeps on saying, 'Ain't peace and quiet wonderful after a lifetime of grubbing for a living?' And I
daresay it is, but I want some new clothes or at least
a look in a shop window, and a cinema, and having
lunch in places where you see the passers-by. And
then he gets all funny about prices and says all I
want to do is spend, spend, spend, it's a good job
someone's growing lettuces.

Well I'm as fond of home-produce as the next, but
this ridiculous; I'm too young to go to early grave.
Still, it's his birthday next week, maybe we'll have
celebration then.

Took little blu pass book down to town on bus with
me and bought him birthday card and gardening
book (big section lettuces) also large-check shirt
and then on impulse, cowboy hat like DULLARSE,
which he watches.

He furious. No Happy Birthday after all. Told me
I should have saved the money and we couldn't

go to the pub now for two weeks. I furious back and called him mingey, cheese-paring sod. Wore the cowboy hat myself when we went up the pub (he calmed down later and very sorry for what he said, explaining he always worrying about money) but I might just as well not have bothered. Nobody looked at me except Callum and he just nodded.

Nobody noticed the cowboy hat at all.

Called Amy to say come up quick and visit, you'll never recognize Fatgirl now and she say never mind the cat, what about you and Stan?

And I said he not slim yet but come anyway, laughing, and then I asked how things were in South Norwood, feeling very homesick, and she told me. And after we done all the relatives and aquaintance I asked (lightly) if she'd seen Sharon slag.

She told me married and in pudding club.

Suddenly my lips went all cold and stiff. Started to ask Amy how she knew, but realized; if that bitch noticing, she must of fallen for the baby five, six, seven months ago. Said hurriedly to fill the lengthening pause, 'How soon can you come up?'

And then I put the phone down and stood breathing and thinking hard.

Should have asked when slag got married and who to and *how* big now and things like that.

Went upstairs to bedroom and sat down on bed. I remember the sunlight come in slanting and fell across the floor in squares. Thought how the room, being very old like rest of house, had probably seen woman blubbing over something a man done before.

Bloody fucking sodding bloody stupid men!

Dried eyes, reapplied mascara. Went down and

told him Roderick and Amy coming up on visit, and he said oh good, when, and wassup with you, got 'eadache or summing? Let's have a cup of tea.

Couldn't sleep that night. Lay awake listening to distant sound of sea. Always drown meself, I supposed. And her.

Still! Think, 'Reen — Slag like the Countess, probably had hundreds of men. Anyone of them could be the father of her coming child.

Dozed off, a bit comforted, then suddenly wide oh very wide awake.

Isn't there something called *genital fingerprinting* these days?

The McKays arrived and fell about in admiration at the house. Left the FIRE LX outside too, in case they'd forgotten that.

R. said, 'Congratulations, Porky. You've really done it this time. Place looks like something out of a brochure advertising rural England.'

Amy said, 'I've never seen anything so picturesque in all my life.'

We sat out later and she admired all my garden furniture, and noted gnomes happy again, grouped round big red stand light I got to go by pond.

'Gnomes got *knocking shop*?' R. said, eyebrows raised.

A bit indelicate, I feel.

Amy said she should have brought video camera and I told her surprise, we got one coming tomorrow with Wayne, Dorelia and the baby, because of course they film her all the time. She's trying to crawl. And Amy said a forward child indeed and when she taking her M.A.? And we all laughed.

What a weekend. The baby come and tried to crawl and everyone on film, even Stanley shouting

'Fuck it!' when he burned his hand on the barbie. Still, Sunday evening they all had to leave and day-glo tubular chairs stood about the lawn looking all empty with bruised grass and marks of feet and dropped bits of burnt liver which our Fatgirl found.

And then too, of course, the memory of what Amy told me about Slag returned.

Monday, it rained stair rods all day long. Knocked me fuschias about. In the evening he said, 'We'll go up the pub.'

Made a change.

'Who we going to talk to, then?' I asked and he said if locals snotty, their hard cheese.

Made me smile.

Really pissed off though and sat there with Cinzano and bag of crisps and couldn't smile. Then the door opened and that Callum come in.

We'd seen him earlier that day down the town, must have had ten-twelve-fourteen girls all round him, hanging on his arm, pushing and looking up at him. He seemed to be feeding them all chocolate bars, bit of a contrast to that Skinny and his teenage whores at home.

S. said all contemptuous, 'Local stud.'

Envy, thy name is Stanley Spink.

Well, I got into the Cinzano and after a bit I chatted to Callum and informed him his Dad had a face like a Viking.

He asked most politely if the Vikings were a London group and I felt dead embarrassed by his ignorance. I explained and his face cleared and he smiled.

'Yeah,' he said. 'There's been ugly sods round here for bloody years.'

I thought we were getting on quite well but he

suddenly remembered he got to go poaching by the light of the full moon and I was left feeling snubbed. I mean, he might have wrapped it up more gracefully about his cooking. Nobody poaches anything by the light of the . . .

'Oh Stanley, I am a fool,' I said.

'I already knew.'

Poaching, see? More'n one kind. *Not* cooking. Oh 'Reeny.

Feeling randy and S. can't or won't oblige.

Tried most of what I knew last night including pretending it a Mars Bar. Weren't no use measuring it for size the way we used because it only makes him more and more depressed.

A flicker once and he all keen to go ahead but everything down again and so is he.

'You were trying to run before you could walk,' I told him.

'Just standing up would be achievement,' he said gloomy.

He all apologetic later, waiting for me to say 'Bet you managed it with Scumbag,' but I didn't. I was just glad my feeling had come back even though there was sodall I could do about it. It had been a bit like lights going off one by one in darkened room, you don't notice it at first. Then you think 'Where am I?'

So it was with me – I hardly noticed going off our Stanley but the Damart vests, the 'Give us a bit!' and the continual raspberry tarts, not to mention his socks, all added up. It was gradual, though. He didn't present me with them all at once.

Seesaws, innit, a classic case. All that time I spend avoiding him, going to bed with 'eadaches, saying 'Be quick and get it over with, then!' must have been a right old turnoff for him.

Well what goes down must come up again.

I hope.

And adding to his depression is no noble relatives come to claim kin with him as I know he hoped they might once we got up here.

Told him, 'How could they? You think they even know that you're in Norfolk? They haven't got osmosis like that Dr Spock. How can they turn up and embrace the missing heir if they don't know you're here?'

'I thought we'd meet them acidentally by now,' he said. 'Me features stand out in a crowd, I know. I thought someday there'd be a huge, glad shout of recognition somewhere . . .'

'In The Red Lion, perhaps?'

'Well maybe not there. But me features do stand out, don't they?'

'Oh, they stand out alright,' I reassured him. 'They been standing out for years.'

'There's no need to be so sarcastic,' he said, huffy.

Well, I ask you. And he makes fun of me for reading Romance!

He further down than ever. Only Fatgirl and lettuce doing well on our plot.

Does he miss Sharon Trainshop? And could she make him get it all up, up, up and away?

Brooding.

Also this secret knowledge that she heavily pregnant bothering me. But shan't tell him yet — if ever.

Into Norwich by omnibus, all on my own. Asked

him, 'You coming?' But he got lettuces to see to.

They got lovely big shops and busy market in Norwich, also museum, better than Bromley Mall.

The river very attractive in places, the Wensum; lots of architecture and little boats moored under bridges. Mind it isn't the Thames, but then it don't pretend to be.

Homesick, so had to go shopping quickly.

Got back home with a few little purchases and found he hadn't laid the tea which was good excuse to get ratty before he could ask what was in plastic bags. How everything come down to money in the end! It's enough to make you pack up being a green ecofeminist and join the Conservative party!

Well no perhaps not, but I mean.

Big event. Down south to see Dorelia, only one night, Express Coach gets you Victoria in two hours, has reclining seats and videos, also nice little girl coming round with tea and coffee, sarnies and bagsa crisps and even a toilet on the lower deck.

I had cheese and pickle sarnie and bought extra in case hungry later on.

Looking out eagerly, craning neck to see sign posts saying names near home. Cried when coming through the City. Well, Dad born there.

Little Janie cried when I left. Wonderful visit.

Wayne said wistfully, 'Is it very peaceful up there now?'

'Too much so,' I told him.

I had to trot round to Kitchener Close before I left. The Americans had painted *Semper Idem* yellow and chopped out wigelia bush in front garden; the privet hedge had been replaced by white ranch fencing. And our scrollwork on the door all gone and ordinary crisscross grill put up instead.

It was like seeing an old flame dressed in new outfit and not what he wore when pleasing you at all.

Very, very strange. And at the end of journey, Eve's Patch, standing like pretty strumpet in place of lost true love.

Told him the details. Said, 'You should have come!'

'Too depressed for anything,' he said.

'Well I was, coming back,' I said.

'Because of me?'

I didn't answer, and he in heavy, martyrish mood of wet self-pity. Told him later that night I thought we should never have come away. Even Spitalfields where we had one room with Mum in old days, now all Pakki shops and clothing retailers, would be home.

He looked at me a long time and then said, 'Barmy.'

Well, perhaps I am.

'What you on about?' he saying testily next morning. 'Blimey, we got rural paradise up here. Anyone give their eye-teeth for it, and you go moaning on!'

I kept quiet.

'Winter cabbage perking up a treat,' he said. 'Next year . . .'

(Next year?)

'. . . I thought I'd do runner beans, they're easy, dwarf, tomatoes in greenhouse, new potatoes, start at Easter, onion sets . . . Might open a little roadside stall eventually. Bags of money to be made that way. You have awning to protect your stuff, prices on every bag and a tin box with a slit in the lid for money.'

Trusting. But problem of rural violence catching up, even round here.

'If you're worried you could always fit box to stall,' he said. 'But I thought you might like to sit at the receipt of custom – wear a big floppy sunbonnet and chew on a straw.'

Couldn't think of anything I'd like less. Sure, it would give me something to do. But I wasn't that desperate – yet.

'The tits'd come right back,' he said. 'With nothing to do but sit there in the sun.'

'Suppose you'd like me to wear maternity smock and all?'

'Good idea! You got big silly 'at, Moggy?'

Hit him, but without my usual strong feeling. Fed up. Went into Mavis' and bought three Mars Bars. However, they done something to the taste since I went off them and I just couldn't enjoy them like I used. Gave him one. (Mars Bar.)

Then, it being sunny morning, walked out through the flat fields to the little school.

Overtaken at end of other village by beatenup old white Ford van, and while I was looking over the railings, wondering if I got courage to ask if a cleaner's job going, I see this same van parked on a triangle of grass nearby where the road divides. The driver was standing by the railings, like me, watching the children play.

God, he was fat and sweaty-faced. I suppose he was youngish still but it was hard to tell because of him being so fat. The chins on the end of his face went right down to the rest of him without a break. He had greasy long hair in untidy curling little bits and his small piggy

93

eyes were fixed on the children, one little boy in particular.

This blob was trying to get closer to the railings than he was, but that belly stopped him. His pudgy hands were clasped in excitement on the spikes at the top. Made you feel sick to just look at him.

He didn't take his eyes off that playground. Could have been a parent in one of those tug-of-love child cases, sort you see in *News of the World*, but I doubted it.

Just then a handbell clanged, rung by a tall, thin lady in untidy coat, whisps of grey hair escaping from a bun, and all the children stopped running about and organized themselves more or less in groups. It all looked so neat and pretty, the fat gink was out of place and somehow wrong. But then the children and the tall thin woman went indoors and he got back in the tatty white van and roared off, vroom, vroom, vroom, look at me, macho master of the bendy lanes.

This gink was there the next day and the next. He did nothing, only squeezed his wobble to the railings and stood there looking in. But on the Thursday I saw his sweaty hand go through the bars, holding a wrapped sweetie so it stuck out obvious. A little group of boys was playing near and it could only be a matter of moments before one of them saw what was on offer.

In a flash I was right there alongside, saying to those children, 'Don't you know that you must never take sweets from strangers?' And they drew back, all eyes looking up, while Gink made a hurried scramble for his van. He drove off, but I had time to note his number. Then I marched over to the gate and let myself into the playground.

There was a nice-looking, grey-haired woman

in blu overall the other side of the tree, also a much younger one, about as pregnant as it's possible to be.

How on earth had they come to miss the fat man so easily? I was astonished and I spoke my mind. I told them if my child had been in playground while that happening I'd see they were dismissed for negligence. The grey one was flustered, the pregnant one in tears by time I'd finished.

And then out come the Headmistress, the tall, untidy creature with the bun, her glasses all askew and her coat flowing. She was bothered too, and rightly so, being the only qualified teacher on the place, and in charge overall. The other two, I found, were just Nursery Assistants.

Well I'd recovered a bit by this time and said I weren't accusing anyone but problem of someone pushing sweets through railings obviously an urgent one.

'A pusher?' this old bat says, as if trying the word for the first time. 'You surely don't mean drugs? Here?'

'You tell me,' I said. 'I've no proof. But it's definitely not right, even though the children are so young.'

'Oh dear, oh dear,' she says. 'Well, I'll just get my coat. Oh, I already have it, silly me!'

I found out later that her coat her stock response to all emergencies. Unless she had large coat wrapped round her she couldn't cope. When there was a fire once in the School, Pat (that was the grey-haired one) said she had to try to put it out and ring the Service. Miss Pincher (Head) just got her coat.

We went indoors after that and Pat gave me a cup of tea. Meanwhile the children played outside with just the pregnant one to watch them. It worried me.

'I am very much obliged to you, Mrs Er,' Miss Pincher said.

'Spink,' I told her. 'Noreen Spink. I live in Dodderham.'

'Much obliged,' she repeated. 'Still, with the greatest respect, I do hope you are wrong.'

'Oh, so do I!' I told her. 'But with the greatest respect, Miss Pincher, you had better watch out.'

'Oh, I will, I will, I will,' she said warmly. 'But who'd have thought of such a thing round here!'

'There ain't nowhere safe these days,' I said. 'That's all for now, then. I'll be going.'

It never crossed my mind that the 'orrible greasy gink might not be a pusher after all.

And he was proved not to be, as it turned out.

Him and me up The Red Lion in the evening. Callum in there and I told him what happened down the little school. His expression didn't change.

'Yeah, he's been in prison twice before already,' he said, lighting a hand-rolled cigarette.

'For drug-pushing?' The cigarette smelt dry and sweetish.

'Kids. You notice he got all new teeth? One of the fathers caught him before they put him away.'

'You mean he's known?'

'*Chroist*, yes. There isn't a pub round here where he dare show his face. That's why he's got the van and sneaks about round the back lanes.'

And Miss Pincher didn't know that? I wondered. Maybe an old maid like that wouldn't have contact with the net of local gossip, and yet . . . and yet there'd been summing in her face told me she had known, when she'd been talking to me. It was almost as if she'd been protecting Greasy Gink.

'Don't they keep him under restraint, then?' Stanley asked.

Callum drew heavily on his cigarette. 'They used to,' he said. 'But his parents getting on, see? They're busy – with Church matters, cutting the grass in the graveyard, delivering parish magazines. They reckon he's paid his debt to society and . . .'

'Debt to society, my backside!' I said. 'What about all them little kids been through his hands?'

'Right,' Callum said and got up to go. 'If it's any comfort to you, I keep a watch. I'm always looking out for him as I go about.'

'You should have been about last Thursday,' I told him.

'Well you were,' Callum said mildly. 'What's the odds?'

We went home. It occurs to me Miss Pincher, her at the little school, might possibly be aunt or summing to that Gink. Everyone relates to everyone else round here it seems, and S. agrees.

Met his dad in Mavis' shop this morning, little old man bent over like a toad, face seamed in permanent downwards grouch. Well he got things to be downwards grouchy about!

Nipped back smartly into Eve's Patch and slammed door.

Saw Gink's mother today, fat little tiny thing riding huge old bicycle, bending down and up, down and up. She had a jiggly basket on the front, all full of parish magazines. She got off, come into shop and offered me one.

I just backed away in horror.

You given birth to monster, you shouldn't try flogging magazines.

Specially not ones relating to person who on record as being kindly to little kids.

Down the school again today and blimey, there was the white van. Miss Pincher out in playground though and I'd hardly been there two seconds when Callum went roaring past on his motorbike.

Miss Pincher saw me peering over railings and smiled at me and beckoned, so I went in.

'I hear you're looking for a job,' she beamed.

Strewth, they must be *physic* as well as gossipy round here, I thought. Of course it weren't the paranormal, just the gossip. I was to learn that travels faster'n shit on a blanket round here.

'I can clean and wash and mend things,' I said hopefully. 'Also I was a dinner lady, Cranmer Road Infants', two years ago. That's in London. Perhaps you've heard of it?'

She went right on smiling. 'Ever done any nursing, Mrs Spink?'

'Well, I been a nurse,' I admitted. 'Sort of. But only in Old Folks' Home,' I told her, desperate she might see me in her crystal ball. 'Only a auxiliary, really. Didn't give medicines on me own or nothing.'

'I'll tell you why I asked,' she said, tucking up whisps of hair. 'I am looking for a Nursery Assistant. Ideally, of course, she should be trained — N.N.B. or similar equivalent — but I'm permitted to waive the letter of the rule if what the person has is right, qualities of caring and intelligence and so forth. Martha, my present help, is leaving us to have a little baby, you see.'

I couldn't help seeing. Looked as if it would be a pretty big baby in spite of Miss Pincher's forecast. Martha's stomach went 'alf hour before her, like that man (was it Pinocchio?) with the big nose.

I looked at old Pincher and I thought, I got you taped, lady. You want help fast, and you're asking me because you think, Sweeten her and she won't go blabbing about Gink all far and wide.

Cockney mind, see? Quick and shrewd. Oh yes.

'I know all about you,' she said, smiling again. 'I made certain enquiries.'

I could appreciate she wouldn't need computer network.

'I *liked* what I heard,' NATO Intelligence went on. 'And I said to Pat, "She's just the sort of person to fill the post."'

Well when you use words like 'fill the post' to me, I'm a dead sucker. Summing so highfalutin' and office-like about it. Mind you, I think I just rolled up all my competitors by virtue of being able to blow the gaff on Gink at any time, but it's nice to be asked into a job the professional way. I just accepted, though she didn't know that yet.

We went into her little office at the back and talked over what she called my CV. I thought that was funny old French car. But at the end she found me satisfactory for the job without any formal qualifications whatsoever.

Went home cheerful for a change, having promised to come back tomorrow to fill in a contract of employment. And I'm to start with them Monday week, with an option to renew the contract (both sides) in the New Year.

It's only a little school, just the two classes, one of really tiny tots, one of rising fives. After that they transfer to the proper Infants' next to the Junior School on the main coast road. But what a triumph for our 'Reen!

Really chuffed.

*

I always leave the milk out in a jug on the side in the kitchen during day because it makes the tea cold if you put it in straight from the fridge. Also the butter in a dish because of spreading easily. Now he suddenly decided these little arrangements of mine just won't do. Gotta store everything away and have things tidy.

All this terrible, untidy clutter getting on his poor frayed nerves.

Ladida and all delicate, I said. It's only the milk jug and the butter dish, for heaven's sake.

He's not what you'd call a finicky man, only moderately tidy since I trained him — though a far cry from early days of marriage when I used to have to say, pointing to socks on floor, 'Pick 'em up! There's a basket for things like that!' And he, all small-boy-hurt and bewildered, used to say, '*All* of them?' 'Cause that Countess, she indulged him, see? But God knows I ain't picking shitty pants up off of the floor.

So as I say, it's not like him to be crappy over jug of milk and so on left out for a purpose. Going to have to watch this man Stanley for a bit. He's disturbed because he ain't getting any, not that it's my fault this time. He got big black mood coming on though and it's disturbing him and me.

So, casting round in mind for antidote to all this, I went into Norwich where I knew they got lotsa little backstreet boutiques, didn't I.

Hot day. Bought one or two little things; red and white striped wool dress for autumn, drop-waisted, £30.99, marvellous value in a place called *Bangles, Baubles and You Guessed It*, four T-shirts, bargain at fifty quid with the Green logo and *Save the Seals* across the tits, two pair jeans, fantastic money's worth down market, £20.00, and a beautiful cream

100

coloured doubleknit Jaeger cardi with blu anchors on collar and brass buttons at the Jaeger shop in case anyone asks me to go sailing, though come to think of it, I rather doubt they will. Still, you never know. £49.99 only!!!

Also six pair panties, three slips and seven pairs sox, assorted day-glo colours with teddy bear motif which I couldn't resist. They looked as mouth-watering as big sweeties, prettily packaged in shop window.

He out in garden when I got back but I saw him just in time so was able to sneak round the back, whizz upstairs and thrust things under bed before he saw.

'You're back, then,' he said as I come out. 'Don't think I didn't see you. What's the damage?'

'*Damage?*' I repeated, opening eyes wide, wide.

'Don't gimme that,' he said. 'What did you buy?'

'Few T-shirts,' I said truthful and he looked relieved. Still after a few minutes he slumped down again.

'Something on your mind?' I asked. 'I mean particular?'

'Tax bill,' he said, poking at a poor little dandelion with his toe. 'Sodding great big one. Bloody Inland Revenue.' He fished in a muddy pocket and brought out forms.

Oh my God. Or perhaps it should be Owe my God.

£8,000!

'I don't understand it,' he said all miserable and desperate. 'How they get £8,000, for crying out loud? I've always been up to date. And it's got 'E' wiv it. What's that mean?'

'*Extra,*' I said, trying to laugh it off, but no, he weren't in the mood for that. '*Estimate!*' I cried.

101

'That's what it is, they give you estimate on account of not being up with your current position. They 'aven't worked out how much you owe really, being on a pension and things, so they make it all up. Roderick had one of them things after he finished at Safeways.'

'You really think that's what it is?' he said, clutching at straws, all grateful.

'Oh yes!' I said heartily, though I wasn't at all sure. 'They can't never dun you for estimate, Stanley. That's strictly illegal. It's just to let you know they got eye on you up here in Norfolk in case you go getting cocky and say sod you.'

He seemed quite chipper after me embroidering. I hurried in and upstairs and hoiked out all the bags and put them in the bottom of my wardrobe and turned the key and stood there wondering should I swaller it.

I'll tell him later about the clothes, I thought. Sufficient unto the day is the evil thereof. I read that sometime off a Christmas cracker.

I went down and made a pot of tea.

'I got good job coming up,' I reminded him. 'Biscuit?'

'If you like.' He sat down all muddy at the kitchen table.

'Trouble with you is you will go on working out in that hot sun,' I said, putting sweetmeal digestives in a daisy pattern on a Willow Pattern plate.

'It's October!'

'You still got to look out. Did you wear the nice sun block I bought you?'

'Pansy stuff.'

I could tell he was beginning to feel better. Soon he'd be making biscuit joke, if my calculations were correct.

102

'Nothing like a few suggestives in the middle of the day,' he said after three minutes dead. ''Ow about a bit of a lay down to see if the old boy's working today, eh, eh?'

But still no how's yer father. He more depressed than ever.

I joked I wondered if safe to leave him Monday. He gonna blow out his brains?

'No gun,' he said then brightened as he remembered he could probably always borrow one offa Callum.

Toad, little squat father of Gink, in pub tonight. Not many spoke to him, though he raised his cap all around. Wouldn't have surprised me to see he got great ugly warts growing under his hair. His seamed face tried hard to crease itself into a smile all insatiating, but didn't know how. He gimme little smarmy bow, but I ignored him.

I come in rather quick from Mavis' today (Friday) and caught him reading THE DUKE AND EVELINA, must've pulled it out of the middle drawer of the buro. He looked up as I came in.

'*Swanlike neck?*' he enquires. 'You looked at a swan recently?' He ruminated. 'She'd be a sideshow – three, four feet higher than the tallest bloke. Able to poke into all sorts of things.' This idea seemed to please him, and he laughed.

I said tersely, 'Put that back where you found it. You got no business reading that. It's private.'

'What is it?' he asks, all peruviant and nosey.

'A Romance, if you must know.'

'Like old Twice-Nightly?'

'Yes.'

'Well strike a light. You wrote it? Like the rude bits.'

Oh God, I thought I'd trashed all those. I felt suddenly I couldn't bear for anyone to see THE DUKE, it was too private. I grabbed the book from him, smacked his ear and stuffed it in the drawer.

'Now, about these groceries,' I said, for I had him cornered then. 'After the weekend I shan't be here much of the day. You'll have to see to Fatgirl. I'll be back fiveish, earlier if you meet me. So this is for Monday's lunch, this is . . .'

'Hang on,' he said. 'What you mean you won't be here?'

'I told you, dummy. Got meself a job.'

'You mean you won't be here to get a meal in the middle of the day?'

Cor, strewth, if his brains was gelignite they wouldn't blow his head off.

'Look, floparse,' I began, then stopped. Unfortunate term. I took biscuits, tea, butter etc., out of the bag and stowed them away all neat so they wouldn't offend his nerves, then I made a large pot of tea and sat down with me knitting.

'Akky puncture?' I asked, waving needles at him.

But he didn't laugh, only asked soberly if you put boil-a-bags in saucepan gradually or waited till the water really bubbling.

I ask you, what a martyr.

Monday. Walked the mile and a half to the little school. Wore my new drop-waisted, but wasted, ho, ho, as I have to wear an overall, blu nylong, with large, candy-striped pockets.

The building two small rooms with tiny Staff Room with easy chairs connected by sliding door. There's a gally kitchen tacked on one end, and a children's cloakroom with teeny toilets and wash basins up the other. The younger children play most of the time but the bigger ones have organized activities like junk modelling, sorting beads and tiny toys, modelling with clay and flash cards.

At end of first day feeling as if can now write book FIVE HUNDRED WAYS TO ILLTREAT AN EGGBOX, never mind EVELINA.

Pat very pleasant, also Miss Pincher. The pregnant Martha there too, to show me the ropes. There should have been another qualified teacher on the staff, but there's a shortage locally, which is why Miss Pincher is having to make do with just Assistants. What it comes down to, I soon see though, is Assistants do all the work while Miss Pincher flits and dots about.

Still, she handy for collecting dinner money from mothers and playing the piano. When she sings with kiddiewinks she has high, reedy voice like a recorder, drowns everyone else around. Don't know how Martha and Pat keep straight faces when she singing little songs. And it was Pat who coped at Storytime, with nearly thirty children all together, not Miss Pincher.

The day starts by us putting out bricks and sand, wheely apparatus holding trays of this and that, seeing there's enough paper junk around (toilet roll cores, detergent boxes and so on) with rolls of sticky brown paper, pairs of little round-end scissors and the paint pots are full at the easels.

Bad days, Pat says, they do *finger painting* here; all the colours get mixed up on the tables and form a chocolate brown goo, looks most unsavoury, and kiddies draw in it with their fingers. Grownups, fortunately, don't have to touch the stuff, merely place a sheet of paper over it and take a print.

There's dry sand on offer on days when no water play, which Pat says marginally worse than finger painting, from the point of view of clearing up afterwards. And all the time, each day, every day, there are big bricks and little bricks, four rocking horses, two climbing frames, one indoor, one out, a slide in the playground and some swings, two Wendy houses, dressing up clothes, a library corner with some rugs and little armchairs . . .

'At first glance the day would appear to be unstructured,' Miss Pincher explained, and I thought it would indeed because children just arrived at any old time before ten and went to the first activity they fancied. But after ten, I saw, they all had a drink of milk from little coloured beakers and dry rusks to eat, seated on tiny chairs in a half-circle, and afterwards there was toilet training with handwashing and so on and always some singing games and playing percussion instruments before lunch.

A canteen help came in to help cook, but in emergency Miss Pincher had been known to do it, Pat told me, adding, 'God save us all!'

We share a caretaker with the big school in the main road.

This chap was in the little ones' classroom that first morning, fixing large safety fireguard round the Scandinavian-style stove up one end of the room. He looked up when we come in and Pat told who I was but he didn't smile. I don't think men do, generally, meeting a woman the first time. Frightened of giving themselves away or summing. I put him down as just another solid Norfolk dumpling who didn't care much for Londoners coming into the county. He was goodlooking, though.

He wasn't particularly tall but he was certainly bigger than Stanley. Well, let's face it, anybody is.

This one was chunky too, but in an aggressive, unfat sort of way, and dark; brown hair and eyes going just a little bit grey at the sides.

I said goodmorning, civil, and found out his name was Todd. I thought no more about him then except to make up little secret rhyme in my head, thing I'm always doing, whether or not I write it down. Not recording rhyme, not even in this Diary, but will say third line of it ended with 'odd'. He went away after he fixed the guard, no doubt up to the big school to see what wanted doing there.

After lunch everyone had a lay down, the children that is, on little folding beds, just covered by a tiny blanket each, and one of us stayed in the room while the children slept. You didn't pay dinner money if you was doing Sleepwatch, Pat told me and I thought Fine, remembering Inland Revenue after my Stanley like ravening beast.

There was more free play in the afternoon and then a quiet time with a story before going home. Clearing up, after the children had gone, took half an hour, Pat said, so I didn't expect to get home much before five or even half past, what with the walk and maybe a bit of shopping in Mavis' place too.

The local Scouts and Guides use the building two night a week, with the W.I. on Saturdays and a local choir and a Quaker Meet on Sundays, so I supposed that Todd was always kept quite busy. At any rate he seemed to be constantly around in that first week, and whistling very merrily indeed.

Second week. On Sleepwatch Monday. Todd came in to check the fireguard and surprised me.

One little girl was crying for her mum (an hour is a huge long time to try to nap away from home at three year old) so I picked her up, sat her on my lap and let her look at pages in my magazine. Todd went out but then came back to look at guard and looked round as if checking on me, too. I wondered if because you were not supposed to pick the children up if they cried. I didn't care if you weren't, I was sorry for that little girl.

I don't think Todd likes me. He keeps looking at me keenly. Comfort yourself, though, 'Reeny – he's only a poor provincial.

Feeling randy and don't know what to do about it. Yes, yes, I know all about that, and magazines all saying positively *healthy* these days but my grandmother told me I'd go straight to hell if I did and her warning's stuck. Also Stanley says, laughing a great deal, though God knows it ain't really funny if true, it makes hair grow on the palms of your hands.

'Be alright if it made hair grow on the dome of your head,' he said ruefully, fingering the shiny place where he used to keep his little rug. 'There ain't no justice in this sorry world.'

I never thought there was.

He mooching miserably about the place in evenings saying he dunno what to do for company now that I'm out all day. I rather sharply back at him, saying we need the money, and he upset, saying 'Go on, rub it in!' And brooding something chronic.

Five little boys in giant squabble over wooden train today. Tall kid called Aaron Walker won; not a noisy child but very persistent, one of life's winners.

Miss Pincher's attitude to childish quarrels very simple – she just sails out among them, neck going like a chicken's, calling out, 'Play nicely!' Then in

108

again to Staff Room, usually in quest of what's edible. There's often chocolate cake.

I'm putting on weight again. Thought he might notice tits returning like migrating birds, ho, ho, but apparently he hasn't. I mean, he talks keen and is often ready to try to be affectionate, but nothing happens much, so I don't even bother to get undressed these days.

Dear Gramma Purkiss: The Victorians believed in self-help, didn't they?

Pat tell me in playground today that Aaron Walker caught five butterflies last summer term, brought them to school and pulled their wings off under the jungle gym. When she went to stop him he dropped the little bodies and ran away from her shouting, 'Bloody, bloody, bloody!'

The world had better watch out for that child.

My turn again for Sleepwatch. Todd came in after the first five minutes with a spanner in his hand to check the guard. As today fifteenth of October, stoves alight. And I'd put some children's paintings over the guard to dry as the wooden airer for them was full up.

He said, 'Can you take these off? I can't reach the wall.'

I got up and obliged and he grinned. Nice teeth.

Miss Pincher then visible through glass of folding door tapping noiselessly and making urgent signs, looking at me standing there holding paintings as if suspicious – but what of? Todd went away quite quickly after that and I sat down again and folded paintings.

Later when the beds away, she asked me what he had said to me.

Felt like rejoining something flippant, but only said, 'I thought you sent him in, Miss Pincher.'

'Good heavens, no!' she said, giving me a funny look and flicking untidy hair up into her silly little bun.

I opened the Purkiss eyes all innocent. What's so very wrong about caretaker checking fireguard? But then when you come to think of it why did he need to come in with heavy spanner to tinker about just then when children sleeping?

Hmmmm.

And now he getting fussy about what he has for tea.

'Why don't you get something decent?' he complains. 'Summing they don't want from some dustbin somewhere, nut cutlets from the 'elf shop, anything. Anything better than these *turdburgers* you just brought in.'

'That freezer's full,' I told him. 'Up to you to get summing out in time. When I've finished at the school it's too late to go down the town. There's only Mavis and we have to have what she got. Mind, if someone met me with the car or better still did some shopping – like they did when they was off chasing local tart, maybe the meals could improve a bit.'

That shut him up. Referring to that Lollipop always does.

'I don't like it when you're working,' he moans weakly.

Tough.

'Yeah, well I never liked it when you played around.'

'Never gonna let me forget that, are you?'

'No, I don't suppose I am, Stanley.'

'Well, you drove me to it!'

'I *what*?'

'You did. You never wanted me.'

'You wore bloody thermal socks in bed!'

'Better than pink plastic curlers and dirty great thick nighties!'

'Bloody isn't!'

'Bloody is. Anyway, I came back, di'n' I?'

'More's the pity.'

'What you mean by that?'

'You're being childish.'

'So are you.'

'Look,' I said, in effort to stop the boat rocking so much we both overboard. 'Look – I'll do you egg and chips, alright?'

'If you like,' he says, usual answer, and turns away.

Drives me wild.

I got to be nice to him if things are to go on working. It's less than a year he lost that mother of his. Also he left work, must be a wrench in spite of all he says. You need to adjust. And of course he hasn't got woman laughing at his jokes, because buggered if I will after all these years.

Smile, 'Reen.

Got him out and about at weekend, away from that dreary pub. Took a walk along the coastal avoiding stately home of noble ancestors.

But he just moaning that his legs ached.

Pat and me together in playground today. Miss Pincher supposed to be on duty but off indoors eating summing as usual.

Sunny. Leaves turning yellow, no hurry in still Autumn air. Sunlight everywhere, all mellow.

'You really ought to be happy on a day like this,' Pat muses. 'People ought, I mean.'

And then we see that Todd approaching across playground.

'Tea up,' he says, and grins, showing white teeth. 'Message from Miss Pincher.'

'You go,' I say to Pat before I really think. One of us has to stay outside with children. Gink hasn't been around lately, though he's not only reason we keep watch of course.

She goes, but that Todd lingers, his back to the building and its windows. And then as I'm standing facing him he raises his right hand and brushes the back of it against my breast — so quickly that all over almost before I realize.

Well of course, it has to be deliberate. I stare at him and cannot look away.

'Easy,' he says and I wonder wildly for a moment if he's giving his opinion of me. There's no one parked on the green triangle today, no one in the lane. And anyone else adult around is eating biscuits and drinking cups of tea.

'I'd like to fuck you,' Todd says softly. 'I really would.'

And warm, wet feeling in me lets me know I'd like it too and stops me from telling him not to talk dirty.

Miss Pincher then, in coat, still munching and with biscuit in her hand, comes out to take her turn of duty while I go in.

Todd stays talking to her and wild feeling inside me makes me wonder if he's saying ... what he said ... to her. Mind so on him I hardly hear Pat talking until she mentions him by name.

'I said, "He's got a nice line in chat,"' she's saying now. 'That's what Martha fell for.'

'I thought she fell for a baby,' I say, all innocent and big surprise.

Ho, ho, ho.

At home this evening, busily checking on contents of bathroom cabinet when in he comes for a piddle.

'Corn plasters, aspirin, zinc ointment, fly repellant . . .' I mutter. 'Wants renewing. We better take a trip to chemist when we do weekly stock-up.'

'Not many flies about at the moment,' he says, weeing mightily. 'Be more to the point if we got in some big chump chops.'

Oh yes. Those as well. Why not?

Don't seem to irritate so much, his moaning, now.

Tempted. Oh my God I want to.

Surprised, too, by violence of feeling of wanting to score offa him. It would even things up, me going to Todd in a way.

I'm sorry for him of course, but it was his decision to come 'ere – and not my fault noble relatives not popping up out of woodwork everywhere to claim kin.

If he ever was.

Lately, looking at his behaviour, I am inclined to the opinion he the result of parthogenesis,* there couldn't be male equivalent of Countess and just lately S. getting more and more like his mother.

Still, never mind Stanley's virgin birth, eh? I got something very attractive and Hollywood to think about.

* Got that off programme where bloke says started so he'll finish.

113

Sunday. Putting my hair up in French pleat. Have let it grow while here because can't get to hairdresser easily. And that's another thing which riles me, along with the wild bit in the garden. I like things under control.

It suits me, I think, though. Little curls at side.

Made change, too, from that White Satin. Now using Le Jardin d'Amour, young light floral fragrance.

Wanting it so badly, Hollywood style, tonight had to cross legs while TV on and he said all testy, 'Can't you keep still? Stop twitching all about, for Gawd's sake!'

If only he knew.

Gloomy twat.

Second thoughts. Don't think that I can bring myself to do it. And of course there's HIV and AIDS.

On the other hand, as my mother used to say, *wait until you're asked*.

On the other hand, I don't think I can bring myself to do it.

Monday. Into school all cautious, ready to tell Todd to sod off if he tries anything. However, he not there.

Caught off guard, therefore, when he comes into washroom lunchtime when I superintending children at the toilets. Romantic.

He says, all formal like, behind me, ''Morning, 'Reen.'

I jumped and two seconds later felt his hands all warm and solid, wandering over my behind.

Indignant then that he thinks that I'm that easy, particularly when caught sight of Aaron Walker, three washbasins away, staring avidly. Also Miss Pincher come in then, though she didn't get her bottom felt all over.

About five o'clock when clearing up, he was there again. Ignored him this time. Got my jacket, said 'Goodnight, all!' and left.

Lovely October evening. No S. with car. And very soon, footsteps behind me on the lonely road. Todd fell into step beside me and as we come up to a group of trees with a little stream that ran across the road, a kind of ford, he nudged me, and indicated with his head to leave the way.

It was dim under the trees. He took my hand and pulled me further in, to where there was a pine wood with the lower branches all quite dead and there was this brown light over everything, sepia, like old photographs. It was deadly quiet in there. Not a bird sang.

He stopped after a little way and grabbing me round the waist, pushed me up against a tree, holding my hands behind my back. His free hand was fumbling at the top of my dress, trying to get inside.

Then we were flat on the ground, me on my back on the pine needles and there was no more fumbling, just a feeling I thought he might come out the top of me head, he was so big.

Afterwards he sits back and rearranges clothing.

'Oh, you are a lovely fuck,' he says, all Hollywood, but then I'd wanted that, hadn't I, so couldn't complain he didn't sound exactly like my Duke.

It all feels strange now, as I write afterwards. Disgusted with self and feeling little bit sick.

He's fortyish, coupla years younger than me, but what the heck?

'What you got big silly grin on your face for?' he said grumpily when I got in.

'Had a good day,' I told him.

'Well, *I didn't*,' he said, and I thought Thank God, because him being irritable made it easier to handle any diddy bitsa guilt that I got left. If he'd been all soliciting, making toast and meeting me with the car I dunno how I'd be. So go on, Stan, *be* crappy. Be as crappy as you like. Makes me feel whole lot better.

Peeling potatoes at sink and groping in my mind for the memory of pleasure, thinking of Todd's thing. I'm surprised he can't see my glowing mood coming out me hair, me tits, me hands. But he sunk in a thy, if that's the word, watching *Blue Peter Extended Special* and waiting for his tea to come in on a tray.

Cutting chips now and arching back, standing at drainer, as memory of Todd's hands, wandering like . . .

. . . what the Duke dying to do to Evelina, only not had chance (or the bits you need).

. . . what I ain't had enough of.

. . . what they do in Hollywood all the time.

Then that redhaired young man reading Six O'Clock News in pleasant voice, but not as sexy as that Todd's, and just the memory of it enough to set me off again, crossing my legs hard and twisting in me chair.

'You alright?' S. says alarmed. 'Not eating?'

'Not hungry,' I tell him. 'Summing I ate, probably.'

Well, summing I had inside me, that's for sure.

'I see Todd giving you the glad eye,' Pat says when we're putting beds away the next day. A good Christian woman, this one, rather like my dear Sister, only not so clever. Speaks plainly and to the point, though, and I learnt a lot this morning.

'Glad eye?' I said, all flustered and bending down to hide my face. These little metal legs don't always come out easy as they should.

'Oh, it's horrid slang for leering at you,' she says, no doubt thinking Dumb townie cluck, don't know A from a bull's foot. 'He's got a reputation, that one.'

'Reputation?'

She must have thought me thick as Naafi custard, as Stan says.

'He goes after women,' she said, spelling it out. 'I told you he got Martha – er – that way.'

Martha. Oh, yes.

'She's not married?'

'Oh no. But she fell a willing victim to his lust. That's why, when we needed a replacement, I urged Miss Pincher to get someone middle-aged.'

'Gee, thanks.'

'Oh, I don't mean you're not attractive! Dear me, what a stupid thing to say! Of course you are. I think you've got great style – well, more than most round here, anyway. What I really meant was he didn't seem to go for blondes, we thought. Oh dear, I'm just making it worse, aren't I?'

'He hasn't exactly gone for me, as you put it,' I said, lying in my teeth.

She smiled. 'I can see you're a realist, Noreen. It's far better to be realistic, don't you think? Then you don't go getting any false notions about . . . Todd can be very persuasive, I believe.'

Oh, so do I.

'What happened between him and Martha?' I

117

asked her and she looked at me as if wondering if I knew the facts of life. 'I mean, they got any plans to get married or anything?' I had to know.

'Oh no. He refuses to acknowledge that the baby's his. Between you and me, you see, Martha distributed her favours quite a bit.'

'Does Miss Pincher know?'

'Oh yes. She's not entirely the guileless old maid she looks. Martha's behaviour was one reason Todd wasn't dismissed. Miss Pincher simply doesn't know who to believe. And of course, Todd's father was Miss Pincher's cousin by a second marriage.'

Oh, of course.

'Tell me something,' I said to Pat. 'Is everybody related in some way to everybody else up here?'

She laughed and looked at me as if it would be strange if not.

'A great many of them are,' she said. 'Without easy access to this part of the county – remember the Motorway only goes as far as Norwich – lots of people are still living where their forefathers grew up. In living memory you couldn't leave a village to live in another one without being thought of as a foreigner. Some have never been out of Norfolk in their lives. Satisfied with what they have, you see.'

I didn't. To me the thought of never seeing London in a lifetime enough to break anybody's heart. I didn't say so out loud, though, because I suspected Pat of being one of those never left their own village, and of course I can be a model of tact. I pitied her, though. So very far from home.

As for that Todd . . .

They keep herds of cattle in together up here, I mean they have the bull in with all his cows and some are pregnant and some have little calves running by their sides – all one extended family in a

118

field. We come on just such a field one day last July and there was a bull and a cow doing it in the open and everyone else standing around watching as if it the most natural thing in the world. And nobody jealous and pushing for their turn or nothing. Must be the country way.

That Todd reminds of that bull, somehow. (Though must say, when you seen what a bull's got, makes a man look like itty bitty miniature in a dolls' house by comparison.)

'Of course *his* wife took Martha's pregnancy rather hard,' Pat went on, musing. 'His ex-wife, I should say. Round here, though, you'll find they don't take much notice of divorce. Once married, always tied, we reckon. In the towns,' she went on, making divorce sound like mains gas, not connected to the villages, 'they pay more attention, I expect.'

I put all this on mental disc and stowed away. And that Todd showed up again after work, same time, same place and same Batchannel.

He wanted me naked this time. I said it was too cold. (Though the body better than some young, if I do say it myself, and the tits beginning to come back, as earlier recorded.)

We argued, and in the end I just peeled me blouse back − and felt a triffic feeling of *This is where I came in.*

I have been here before, like the lovely poem says, I thought. And I remembered.

It was our Stanley, thirty year ago in Cudham, Kent, saying, 'I only want to look, 'Reen Purkiss. No harm in that, is there?'

And me with everything under wraps − circle-stitched, Marks and Spencer cones, jutting out and slightly sideways, like the guns on James Bond's car.

119

Yes, this is definitely the place in the film show where I came in.

Then I thought, Glory Hallelujah, you fool, you should be giving thanks. I mean, when it all does come to an end – and I don't suppose there'll be many asking to see my tits when I'm seventy – then you'll know show's over and nothing to do then but go home, roll over and shut eyes for ever.

It weren't quite so instant as yesterday, I had time to feel it going in.

'Alright?' he asked, pausing. Closest I ever came to talking to him.

I gasped and shifted my behind.

After that you might say he forgot that I was there – in person, that is, he knew my fanny was. He didn't make much noise – and I was on Cloud Nine as we used to say, when he finished. I never had time to think about other things – paying Stanley back or disease or nothing, I was just *happy*, looking up at the yellow-green leaves above me and seeing mellow sunlight and hearing somewhere, a robin start up little trilling song.

Todd sat up and took a packet of Rizlas from the pocket of his jacket lying by us on the ground. Then he rolled us each a cigarette, filling the papers from a pouch, and I noticed the same dry, sweetish smell that hung around Callum.

'Ground poppy heads,' Todd said. 'Dried broom and Damiana. I roll my own. Not working to keep the tobacco industry in new drawers.'

'Don't tell me. You're related to Callum.'

'Only by adoption. Wanna get high?'

We smoked and I felt – not high, but peaceful. Then we dressed and I went home to see what sort of lamb chops our Stanley had got in for tea.

*

120

About three in the morning woke up worrying about AIDS. In America, I know, you have to have a certificate to do it now.

Lovely, happy mood and feeling of wanting it no matter what, quite worn off and sneaky feeling of disgust come back, also quite a bit of unease. Sex used to be something that I did with Stanley.

Couldn't sleep. About four got up and went and had a bath. He didn't stir.

Dorelia, Wayne and baby up this weekend.

'You're looking different, Mum,' my daughter said.

Different? All I can say is Thank God Amy didn't come with her perceptive eyes.

'New shade of blusher?' D. goes on. 'Or is it just sea air?'

'Sea air,' I said, but I could feel her gaze following me as I got the tea and laid a table.

S. had piled logs from a tree Callum had cut down either side of the ingle nook. (We done away with the Magicoal in the end, it looked so silly.) Now he threw on another branch or two and it crackled and spat sparks; it was Ash, you can burn them still green.

They stayed the afternoon and part of the evening, leaving about nine. And often when I raised me eyes, there was that daughter of mine looking at me all expectoratively. Not nice.

'Alright?' he asked me later, 'cause he knows I'm usually down after D.'s gone home, and I nodded. I was more than alright, I was alive and wanting it again, early morning gloom completely gone. Must be summing to do with the time of day, I thought.

'You chipper now, or what?' he asked again.

'Oh, I'm chipper, right enough,' I said.

He looked at me and grinned. Well, his face changed.

'I wasn't going to say anything until I was sure,' he said.

'Don't then,' I told him, wondering what the hell he was on about.

'But – well, 'Reeny Spink, I think your luck just changed,' he said.

'It did?'

'Don't count your chickens.'

'Eh?'

'*Chickens*. Hint, hint, hint. Oh blimey, Mog, you are dense! The old *cock*.'

'What about it?'

'Fings are looking up. Well one of 'em is. I was watching a rerun of that holiday programme after you'd gone to bed last night and . . .'

'Let me guess.'

'Do you want to hear or don't you?'

'I'm listening.'

'Well, that's it, really. It just sort of stirred as I was sitting there. And I said to myself, "Eh? Eh?" Because it was like remembering something I had forgotten. And you know what the worst thing about it all was? Pay attention, Moggy! The worst thing was I suddenly realized I hadn't even known that I'd forgotten. How about that?'

'That's not the worst thing that could happen.'

'No?'

'The worst thing ain't you realized you didn't know that you'd forgotten, but that your partner knew and didn't tell you.'

'Eh? You mean you knew about me all the time?'

'Only as much as you knew about me not knowing I'd forgotten what I suddenly remembered I'd not realized.'

122

'Stop winding me up! This is serious!'

'So was my going without,' I told him. 'I just about got adjusted to it. I'm not sure I can manage it tonight. And anyway I think I got a 'eadache.'

Why is timing nearly always so disastrously out in relationships? The Spink sex seesaw about level now, but here's me wanting to upset it badly. We got chance to mend things, patch all up for ever and all I can think of is: It's my turn to play.

I don't hate Stan. I don't. But something in me wants to hit him hard. And other, grubby little something wants to keep having it off with Todd until I'm tired.

I never really seen my way so plain before. I want what I want and I'm going to have it. Is that the way a man thinks? I don't really care.

It's nice making up your mind and not having to give in to no one. I mean, when you're married you gotta consult, even about the wallpaper for the breakfast nook, but when you're single, or even single-minded, you don't give a toss. I know my widowed Aunt Florrie, and she's not the only one, been heard to say she'd never get married again. Mind, she's living now with my Aunt Vi . . .

But that, as we say in Romance, is a whole different kettle of baby.

Sunday. Busy sorting beads to go with frocks and blouses. Then occurred to me Todd more concerned with what underneath, so fished out the fancy underwear I got in Norwich on last trip.

Shall have to let the new things trickle out piecemeal as it were; he raises eyebrows enough times as it is at prices and I have to say, 'What, this old thing? I had it fifteen year.'

May I be forgiven.

Thursday. Woken from disturbing dream Claire Rayner come to warn me about catching AIDS, even though using barrier method of contraception, to find something even more disturbing going on outside. Tinkle and thud and crash of broken glass, though not the Scarecrows' door this time, but greenhouse.

Out of bed and over to window to look out.

Blimey, things flying about just everywhere; you never saw such wind.

He sitting up now, bleary-eyed and saying, 'For Gawdsake shut that window!' And I ask awed, 'What is it, Stanley?' And he say, 'I dunno, do I?' – all irritable and mystified, getting out of bed and padding over to where I am to have a look.

It had been raining and the telephone wire was dancing excited outside, gleaming in the light from the bedroom window. Pine trees in the wild bit sighing as if bending double.

'Oh, me greenhouse!' he cried out as another crash and tinkle. 'Oh shit, me greenhouse!'

He shuffled quickly into dressing gown and slippers and ran off down to see. And presently he come back, gloomy and fed up but with summing else behind his eyes as well.

'I never seen anything like it,' he told me. 'It's a hurricane. One apple tree knocked sideways on the kitchen wall, the greenhouse roof stove in. Mavis' fence, where it touches ours, is down, and there's old chimneypot lying in the road.'

'I'll make a pot of tea,' I said.

Well we had no more sleep that night, and in

the morning Mavis come in early to say no power in shop because lines all down for miles and he said that he *told* Eastern Electric summing like this would happen on account of having all that knitting strung about on poles and not underground like in London.

There was a pine tree oddly leaning over down the garden and some shrubs and little trees wholly uprooted. What wind force strong enough for that, I wondered, and how widespread? We couldn't even get TV to find out, though later Mavis produced a radio with batteries and we heard it all over southern coast and London.

About nine began to make my way to school. Trees right across road in places and had to climb over. Thought to myself, This'll stop Gink's farting in church for a bit.

However, no school today; huge branch of chestnut tree in playground fallen against windows. Miss Pincher – in coat – Pat, Toad and assorted mothers, fathers and children standing around surveying damage, and awaiting Fire Service lifting gear which will arrive God only knows when, having, presumably, many more urgent calls on its time.

Wind dropping; having done its worst, about to bugger off to Continent. Good; about time the rest of Market had its quota. Meanwhile, nothing to be done, not even chance to talk to Todd alone.

Pat said to me, nodding towards Miss Pincher, 'This is surely a three-coat problem.' And when I didn't quite get what she meant, said, 'Sherlock Holmes.' I said I didn't read detective stories.

Still, if ever occasion called for a coat, it's now. Miss Pincher flitting about, examining damage and

125

exclaiming in high, reedy voice that it's terrible — in case anyone hadn't noticed, I suppose. She's shooing mothers and children out into the road, and tucking hair and grabbing coat, which keeps rebelling and trying to get away, and is altogether in her element. Ain't had so much excitement since her periods started.

Home to find him moodily clearing up greenhouse.

'They had it worse elsewhere,' he says with satisfaction. 'Insurance going to have to pay up. They gonna get me a new greenhouse for a start.'

The power come back on in afternoon and we got the News. Pictures of Sevenoaks with trees lying all around like matchsticks. Made me cry.

He said, 'You going to cook the tea or what?' And I looked at him with disgust. Right now that Sharon Trainshop could have him and right welcome. No wonder she wanted out. No delicate feelings at all, except towards his bloody greenhouse.

Up pub, where locals talking animated, well, animated for them, about the Gale and its damage, swapping stories and vying with each other who had it worst. Toad not up there, nor Gink, neither. Here's hoping that both got hit by flying trees.

Then Callum in to say, 'You *seen* him?' — not to us but to people by bar, and some heads nod and talk turns from Gale to Gink.

'Face gone for ever,' Callum says, amused. 'Lips split open, one eye dangling out on thread.'

The others smile, then seem to be aware of us in corner and it's heads together, voices reduced to rumble.

Stanley goes up to bar for further pint all nonchalant, with ears pinned back. Bunch of mothers set about Gink, it seems, not for anything he done special, but for being what he is and threatening, looking at the children turned away from school.

And were those women prosecuted? I could have given Stanley answer before I asked him. Gink crawled away afterwards, watched by certain representative of the Force – presumably to make sure he hadn't been actually killed – and the women not even cautioned, as one of them – wait for it – the daughter of the nephew of the Sergeant down the town Nick.

We wonder, the two of us, where Gink crawled to – Toad Hole where warty daddy lives, no doubt. Couldn't very well try local hospital – only too obvious there'd be nurses there related to children he's favoured with attentions in times past and who'd be glad to make his wounds worse instead of better. Me, I'd pull them wide, wide open. I should like to hear him scream.

Home again, then, down and not even squiffy. And we didn't know it then but that was the last time we was to patronize that particular public house – indeed, that or any other for a long, long time to come.

Saturday. No school all week. Out for walk with Stanley. Saw a pub called The Fat Ox and said to him, 'Hey, look – they named one after you!'

He laughed at first, but later said rather bitterly, 'Ain't oxen just castrated bullocks, though?'

Still, little later, sees a sign by side of road, saying *Dressed Crabs* and feels strong enough to say a little summing about how he hopes they got all new fashion gear and not topless, so he must be feeling better.

And at home he resurrects old song.

> 'We're having a bit tonight!
> Mother says I must be quick
> To get me fill of spotted dick.
> I love my roly-poly,
> It fills me with delight,
> Haven't had a bit since Easter,
> We're having a bit tonight!'

But are we? That is the question. I get into bed and find it's all brag with him. He was the one who was counting chickens. The old cock don't really want to know.

Into town. And I see this green T-shirt in *Granny Wouldn't Like It*, which this granny liked very much indeed. It was £20, marked down from £29.95, a bargain if ever I saw one, and I simply couldn't resist. It has *Morston Marshes Mountain Rescue Team* printed across the boobs and a picture of someone swinging from a rope. How he moaned about purchase! I felt very much better for it, though.

Also, having finished little dress I was knitting for Janie for the winter I bought new knitting pattern and wool in bright blu twisted-knit for bobble hats and mittens for us both, husband and wife look-alike sets. He weren't much impressed with that one, either.

Weather chilly today and cold wind from the sea. Lettuces over. I thought they was eternal.

There was summing on TV tonight about the Stock-market crashing, but I didn't pay much attention, being closely involved with my bobble hats and counting stitches. He come down from a bath and said, 'Anything on box?' And I said, 'Nothing much, don't bother me, I'm counting.'

He then asked, 'Ready for an early night?' And I said, 'I'm *counting*. You wanted little bobble hat for your little bobble head, so I'm doing it. Push off.'

He said, 'I'm not all that keen and never was, and I'll think we'll just look silly.'

And I was furious and said, 'That all the thanks I get, knitting my fingers to the bone?' And he said, 'Oh, alright then!' all sulky, and went up to bed.

I sat on for a bit, but I still couldn't get the thing right, so thinking I must be tired, I left it and waiting until I thought he was asleep, went up to bed too.

I turned the TV off first, of course and pulled out the plug. It was all extra programmes, a lot of coming and going and 'We interrupt this to bring you . . .' and things like that, but I didn't stay to watch. I mean, the Beeb gotta have summing to fuss about or it got no life, whether it's open-heart surgery, Save the Whale or dirty food. No, as I say, being tired, I left all and went to bed. I said to myself that everything would look quite different in the morning.

And it did.

Letter come this morning from our friendly Financial Adviser, sweet little roses man in London with heading *Hibernian Unit Trust Valuation*, and lots of good stuff about high level of liquidity, bids and seculation, hard landings and growth forecasts. But the main message, though it all wrapped up in phrases, was *Regret*.

He regretted a great deal, our friendly man.

I didn't bother reading the letter through because look on Stanley's face told me what it got to say

– our usable income's been cut by about a third. I thought of all the pretty clothes upstairs and the way I'd left the immersion heater on and my pig-outs on chocolate and felt cold.

But he was savage.

'They can't do this to me!' he cried. 'We come up here on their advice . . .'

'It was your idea.'

'They said it would be cheaper!'

'Well, they didn't know, they couldn't of foreseen this crash. It has to be a one off, doesn't it?'

'Bloody hope so,' he said. 'Have another one, we won't have no capital at all. I told you and told you not to go buying all those clothes.'

'I got to have something.'

'Not out here you don't. You don't *need* them out here.'

'What've I got to do then, go round looking like some muddy vegetable you just dug up?'

'No, but there's a limit, there's a *limit*, 'Reen. You're just gonna have to see. There's to be no more little trips to Norwich raiding them boutiques and things.'

'I don't . . .'

'You do. Don't think I haven't seen them plastic bags. Well, now we're skint,' he said with satisfaction. 'You're just going to have to make the whole lot last.'

He waddled off to greenhouse or what left of it and I raised two fingers at him as he went. Snooping little bugger. Made you wonder what else he knew he shouldn't.

Don't need no new clothes, eh? Might as well be dead.

What's he got in mind for us, that's what I should like to know. Getting older and shabbier in this

130

dump with no friends and the Family all miles away? Depression come down and settled closely on me. I could of built my coffin, jumped right in and pulled down lid.

Oh bugger him. And Goddamn and blast the international Stockmarket to everlasting fiery hell.

It was the Yanks who started it. Colonials! They never should have broke away. I never met a Colonial yet with the sense they was born with.

After a bit I cooled down and then that Mavis come in. Made a pot of tea. Moaned to her about money and she moaned right back.

'Mind, you won't hear of it affecting *them*,' she said, nodding her head towards the window and meaning villagers. 'They're all like *that* round here.' And she hooked the third finger of one hand over the index finger and held the hand up. Looked just like two dogs mating to me. She got outside a large slice of Mocha cake I made and went on, 'You won't get no sympathy from *them*. You tell 'em you're selling up and they'll just say "Good. Hope Norfolk person gets your house next time."'

'We're not selling up!' I cried. 'What — sell Eve's Patch?'

'I didn't mean you,' she said. 'I meant the Stores. Still, you could get quite a bit for your place, you know, with house prices rising so fast. Tell you something confidential. I've just had an evaluation on the Stores and it's double what I paid two years ago.'

'Get away.'

Well she went home soon after that and I got Stanley a snack lunch. Didn't feel like one meself, must've been full up of Mocha cake. We had the News on, they always give you the state of the City at the end.

131

I had to turn the sound up quite a bit because S. got plate of hi-baked water biscuits, cheese and juicy, crunchy apple, but sense of ongoing market panic loud and clear even without the sound.

'Oh shit,' he said, spitting biscuit flakes. Then he got up and turned lovely Moira Stewart off and we sat in silence. Well, what I really mean is neither of us spoke. He still had some biscuits left.

'I dunno,' he said at last, summing up for the two of us. 'Wait and see, eh?'

'Yeah, why not?' I said and got up and took the last biscuit away from him because I couldn't bear his crunching any more.

Later I walked out along the lane to school.

The area deserted except for men up on the roof. No sign of our Todd. Walked back alone and thoughtful and met Callum, carrying his ferret bag.

Asked him how Gink was, just to make conversation, and his face closed up.

'Where does he live?' I asked curiously. 'In The Square?'

'Nah!' he said scornfully. 'Only Norwich yuppies live in there. Real old Norfolk live in council houses these days.'

'You got your ferrets with you again,' I said brightly, and he nodded. 'Do they bite?'

'Nah. Soft as bloody muck. But if they did – know what you got to do? Only two ways to make a ferret let go – snap it on the snout or else squeeze its gut. They don't like that.'

'What do they eat?'

'Dog food, birds, mice, anything as long's it's meat. Not starlings, though. Something in the brains of a starling'll kill a ferret.'

Learn a little everyday, say I.

I said, 'Well, see you, then,' and he said, 'See you,' all casual and strode off whistling, the ferrets over his shoulder, bumping and wriggling in the bag.

Monday. Back to school, with Miss Pincher permanent in coat.

Two things missing though: great hanging branch of chestnut tree in playground and the caretaker. One gone for firewood and the other . . .?

'Flu,' says Miss Pincher, giving me sharp look.

I bet she knows all. I really feel resigned to that, because probably he's her third cousin on auntie's side by tenth marriage as well as his father being her cousin by a second.

'They give me feeling of claustrophobia round here,' I tell him in the evening. 'All this gossip. If you went to Norwich to buy new drawers they could tell you how much lace they trimmed with before you get off the bus.'

'Exaggerating.'

'No I'm not. They're just a close-knit bunch of scandal mongers, all related.'

'Depends what you got to hide,' he said, shaking out *Daily Mail*. 'You got summing special?'

'No.'

'Shouldn't bother you, then.'

'It doesn't.'

'Well, then.'

'I mean, how could it? We got no secrets here.'

'No.'

'Let them gossip, I say.'

He sat up and gimme look over the edge of his paper. 'Moggy, you worried about them finding out we ain't so rich after all?'

'No. We can't help that, if it's the truth.'

'What you worrying about then?'

'Just *things.*'

'Women!' he said, diving into the depths again with rustling noise. 'You shouldn't be so touchy.'

'I am not being touchy!' I shouted at him.

And he sighed.

November. Leaves falling fast. Well, I always knew they did, but somehow you notice it more up here.

Foggy. Summing they call 'sea fret' blowing in from sea. Trees out of sight up end of garden. He took me in to school.

Not a sign of Todd – and hasn't been since the Gale. Relief caretaker in. I daren't ask too many questions – if I did, probably find the whole neighbourhood knew what I done, with whom and where and how long it took. And I can feel Miss Pincher watching me.

She is really soppy beyond belief where the characters of children are concerned. Mind, that's better than wanting to molest them, like some round here, but she not inhabiting same world. In fact when it come to choosing little people for parts in annual Christmas Nativity Play, she acts as if from totally different planet.

She wants that Aaron Walker for the part of Joseph.

Now Nativity Play, Pat tells me, is important local event each year, with three performances at least and more if Miss Pincher can pressgang local people in. There's one for the fond parents, one for the Old Folks (compulsory attendance) and one special gala do for town councillors, school governors, local magistrates and any other lavatory attendants left over from other times.

134

And so, as Play to take place in first part of December, we got to start shaping it now; learning carols, talking about story so children well-informed and everyone think Council money well spent on pre-school education and Miss Pincher working her butt off and most worthy.

But – Aaron Walker for the part of Joseph? Pat turns to me with surreptilian wink, meaning lotta work to be done there, for starters.

Miss Pincher, tucking up hair, leads off by saying she feels strongly that what is needed is freshness. A Nativity Play needs freshness. Also spontaneity.

We agree. At least, Pat nods seriously, no doubt hiding the fact that she's heard the freshness and spontaneity bits before.

'I feel strongly,' Miss Pincher goes on – which is Pincher-speak for 'This is the way we're going to have it' – 'that as Aaron Walker is such a nice, big child, he would do splendidly for the part of Joseph.'

'He's certainly big,' Pat says, and I keep quiet, being new to the proceedings.

There's a little, thinking pause.

'How about Pippa Jones for Mary?' says Pat, that old hand at campaigning with Miss Pincher.

The old girl pencils initials 'P.J.' pensively on piece of paper on table before her and it's left to me to suggest mildly that maybe Teddy Bures, Aaron's best mate, would also be a suitable candidate for Joseph.

'But what about Aaron?' cries Pincher, clasping her hands and trying to look democratic.

'Oh I think he would make a perfectly splendid Innkeeper!' Pat says, also clasping her hands, to show sincerity. Personally I thought she was over-doing it. Aaron out was what we wanted, not merely

135

a down-grading to Innkeeper. Then I thought, Oh sod it, and I clasped my hands as well.

The Aaron-for-Joseph faction was outvoted two to one.

'Very well,' says Miss Pincher, doodling little boxy houses on her list. (Surprised she doesn't draw coats.) She still feels strongly Aaron should have a starring role, though, and we give in. Should just be thankful she hasn't nominated him for Gabriel, I suppose.

'I don't think we need bother with the Anunciation,' she says hurriedly and slides quickly on to the question of which battered dolly in school collection is best for the Baby Jesus.

Brief discussion about whether Jesus dark haired or not, and then we settle for old, bald doll done up in bandages, Miss Pincher's notion of old-fashioned swaddling clothes.

I imagine to myself no live birth scenes on stage, and I am right.

'We'll do the journey to Bethlehem like we always do,' Miss Pincher goes on, making it sound near, like Cromer. She waves the cast list vaguely. 'They'll have left the donkey – somewhere, I expect. Then they knock at the door of the Inn – that'll be the Wendy House facade – and the Innkeeper opens unto them. Extempore dialogue, of course. Must have freshness and spontaneity. You can't expect four year olds to *learn* dialogue – that is the enemy of all freshness and spontaneity, I feel strongly. When we rehearse we must get them into the habit of saying what comes naturally into their little heads.'

We discuss next a suitable carol to be sung while Mary and Joseph are entering the stable, and the possibility of the Wendy House being turned round

136

at this point so that the audience realizes the next scene takes place in the stable itself.

Sounds a wee bit unlikely to me. Still, who am I to argue?

'Fine, fine,' says Miss Pincher, tucking up hair. 'Any questions, anybody?' — as if she had consultants in their thousands instead of just Pat and me.

There's just a little haggling over the Archangel's speech; Miss P. feels strongly that exception should be made here, with angel speaking traditional lines straight from the Authorized Version and we enquire, just for the look of the thing, whatever happened to freshness and spontaneity? However this soon glossed over and all friends again, Miss Pincher drawing slanting lines of rain falling on boxy houses.

So planning all complete, and I amuse him after tea with telling him.

'She's a typical old maid,' I say.

'Don't kid yourself,' he says. 'Round here? Leave it out. There's no such things as virgins. No — there's many a big prick been up that little fanny, you can bet your arse on that.'

Well, really, Stanley Spink.

I don't think I need to know.

Still no sign of Todd. And we give up going in the pub. S. says gonna brew his own. Oh, Merry Christmas!

He's downstairs now, watching that police programme where they frighten you and then tell you to sleep safely. I'm up here thinking about money and how we ain't never going to be able to go home. If we went back to London now all we could afford is little two up, two down and handkerchief back garden.

137

Later, got up and creamed my face off, did pig and got into bed. He come up with Fatgirl following because she thinks she's human and should sleep with us. He took her down again and then got into bed and we lay there, each down a little well of thought. I was, at any rate.

And then he leaned towards me, all eager, wanting it and I thought, It could be Todd there in the dark. One whanger like another, after all, and each got little person on the end.

And everything come right because I was pretending he was Todd.

And he was really chuffed when he fell back, panting on the bed.

Children all keen to sing, but nothing can make them sing the right words.

> '*Away in a manger, no crib for a bed,*
> *The Little Lord Jesus lay down his wee dead . . .*'

Aaron Walker sneering openly at acting; he knows all about it on account his mother in W.I. drama group – and he doesn't think much of it. He's very scornful of Teddy Bures when he puts his arm round Pippa Jones as Mary.

Then Teddy Bures goes all stiff and wooden and the word 'pillock' is heard from Aaron and Miss Pincher gets cross. Plans are mooted to demote him to Last Shepherd, though they're later shelved.

'We'll keep you for the time being,' she compromises, 'but only if you behave.'

Aaron would rather be with the Shepherds anyway, organizing a shoot out with the toy lambs, so this is a silly thing to say.

'Smile,' Miss Pincher goes on to exhort the child.

'Smile. What? Well just look at them as pleasantly as you can.'

Carols to go through next, Miss P. at the piano, pumping away, head thrown back, warbling high in soprano. Children giggle.

Next, everybody's onstage moves. Hiatus then, with the Archangel, Peter Thirtle, and the traditional lines Miss Pincher feels so strongly about.

'Behold, I bring you . . .'

'Good tidings,' prompts Miss Pincher.

'Good tidings . . .'

'Of great joy.'

'Of great joy . . .'

'Which shall be.'

'Which shall be . . .'

'I thought you knew!'

'I thought you knew . . .'

'No, no! I thought you knew the words you have to say, Peter.'

'I do,' says little Peter. 'I just can't remember how they go, that's all.'

'Sock it to 'em, Petey!' Aaron shouts.

'Be quiet!' says Miss Pincher, irritated.

'He's going to muck it up.'

'Will you be quiet?'

'Well he is going to muck it up.'

'Be quiet, Aaron!'

'Well he is. I can tell you now, he is.'

'I said Be quiet!'

'Is,' says Aaron, having the last word.

Miss Pincher takes a very deep and patient breath. Aaron subsides and pinches Pippa Jones so she wriggles and knocks into Teddy Bures, who knocks into Peter Thirtle.

'Aaron!' Miss Pincher says warningly.

'It weren't me!'

'I am persuaded that it was.'

'It weren't! It weren't!'

'Who was it, then?'

'It was him, Muriel the Archangel.'

'*Who?*' says Miss Pincher, hard put to it to keep herself from laughing. And then it is this puddle doth appear, suddenly in the middle of the floor.

Someone didn't ask to be excused. Pat mops it up and we move on, into *Hark the Herald Angels Sing*, which is the signal for the Shepherds to get themselves in order and stop holding woolly lambs by the tails, the better to smite one another.

And lo, the phantom piddler strikes again.

Miss Pincher goes to get her coat, but Pat, preferring to strike at the trouble's cause, grabs hold of Aaron Walker by the arm and shakes him. A plastic water pistol falls from his grasp. Miss Pincher then announces that if this sort of thing goes on we won't have a Christmas Play at all. Aaron seems about to cheer but then changes his mind as Miss Pincher confiscates the water pistol. His lip trembles. Miss Pincher's resolve weakens. She gives pistol back. All sigh. The rehearsal resumes.

But everything will be alright on the night.

Dress Rehearsal. Relief caretaker has arranged six gym boxes from the Junior School in position to make a stage at one end of one room. The folding partition between rooms is drawn back. Clean straw is strewn around the gym boxes for effect of stable, with a toy lamb, separated from the rest of flock, lying solo on back with little legs in air.

To one side of the stage is the Christmas tree, drooping its baubles and tinsel, dark boughs hiding children's presents (for all, *after* the performance), also a large parcel from the children to

140

Miss Pincher – chocolates, what else? Also bath salts and talc for Pat and me, bought by Miss Pincher on behalf of children. We know, because Pippa Jones informed us, in great whispers.

Behind the tree is a folding screen, half-inched by Miss Pincher from local cottage hospital where her sister is a Sister, and behind the screen the little actors will foregather, having tiptoed in from corridor.

At least, that's the basic idea.

The upright piano is on the other side of the room, ready with Christmas music for Miss Pincher to play and sing to and behind are a few rows of folding chairs, put up by caretaker, Pat and me while Miss Pincher reluctantly in playground, supervising children's play in weather that is bleak and grey and drizzly.

In she comes now, strong air of martyrdom about her, rubbing long, thin hands to show how cold it was out there and dying to open the chocolates. Twenty-five children follow her noisily, total numbers reduced by seasonal bugs and things – and all hats and coats and gloves are damp and have to be spread out over radiators to dry.

No water play today.

Lunch next, a makeshift affair, then naptime in which nobody sleeps, being too excited. Lasts three quarters of an hour.

And then the dressing of the dear little actors; the wriggling, the crowns falling off, the surprise – 'Hey, Noreen, it come all undone!' The teatowel-and-rope head dresses drooping on the slant, the elastic of the animal masks going ping! as Aaron Walker pulls them with a finger, the noise . . .

. . . getting on Miss Pincher's shredded nerves.

'Quiet, everyone! Quiet! Must have quiet!'

She stands up and claps her hands and when that doesn't work, places her hands flat on her own head. This looks ridiculous, as a lot of what you do with very small children often does, but it has effect. Everyone copies, including Pat, me and Aaron Walker. It's difficult to be subversive with your hands flat on your head.

Now children in their places, with hands down. Miss Pincher marches to piano. Pat goes to one side of the stage and I go to the other. Opening chord of *Once in Royal David's City*. Pippa Jones and Teddy Bures come up the far steps over by Pat. On my side Aaron Walker stands as Innkeeper, ready to fling wide the door. I catch his eye and he smiles charmingly.

Mary and Joseph continue to approach.

They knock . . .

And wait.

The Wendy House door crashes back, according to plan. Little Teddy Bures opens his mouth to ask 'Any rooms to let?' or some such phrase, but Aaron pre-empts him. Scowling down at Pippa and Teddy, he moves straight into his part, lively and full of childish freshness and spontaneity.

'Piss off!' this Innkeeper tells Joseph loudly. 'Get out. There's no sodding room inside.'

'But what are we going to *do*?' Miss Pincher wails. 'He's not – he's just not dependable.'

'Oh, he is, Miss Pincher. You can depend on him for anything,' Pat says grimly.

'We can't – er – *sack* him. It's far too late for that. Did you talk to him, Pat?'

'Oh yes, Miss Pincher. But all he said was "You told us to say just what came into our heads." He was all aggrieved.'

142

'He knows,' Miss Pincher says darkly. 'He knows.'
She's well wrapped in her coat by now and her hair
is coming down like crazy. 'And tomorrow we have
the parents coming and oh! What shall we do?'

I venture to put in a word. 'I have an idea,' I offer
cautiously. 'Though I don't know if it'll work.'

Miss Pincher seizes wildly at this straw.

'Have you, Noreen? You have my full, free permission to try anything with that child, within the
usual limits, of course.'

I do have an idea. And the next morning I take
Aaron Walker on one side.

'You know we are to act the play for the mummies
and daddies today, Aaron.'

'Yeth.'

'Well, you're still the friendly, caring Innkeeper,
in spite of using those words yesterday.'

'Am I?'

'What are you going to say to them this time when
Mary and Joseph come knocking on your inn door?'

'What I think of, like Miss Pincher said.'

'You mean you're going to use those words again?'

'I might. If they come along first, I got to. Miss
Pincher said.'

'Miss Pincher didn't mean that you should use
those words.'

'Oh. Well, she might have told me.'

'Aaron – listen to me very, very carefully. If I hear
you use the words "piss" or "sodding" this afternoon, I shall personally smack your little bottom
hard. Do you understand?'

He looks at me, the words 'On stage or off?'
trembling on his lips.

'You promise not to say "piss" or "sodding"?'

He nods.

'Right. You can go and play now. But Aaron . . .

143

Try to be a *nice* Innkeeper. Make Mary and Joseph feel wanted, even if all you can give them is a stable. You're friendly and caring, not cross and horrible.'

He runs off and I have a quiet glow of pride.

'Settled it!' I tell the other two. 'He's *promised* not to use those words.'

'Oh, thank goodness!' poor Miss Pincher cries.

Afternoon comes and the mothers file in between the rows of folding chairs, together with a sprinkling of fathers, grandmothers and babes-in-arms.

Quiet. Salvation Army tape of carols playing softly. Pine smell of Christmas tree mingling with smell of school. Atmosphere of hushed expectancy, mothers craning necks to see little darlings in earliest second of appearance. Miss Pincher goes importantly to the piano.

Once in Royal David's City plunked out and children slow to sing until encouraged by Pat and me. Audience must think this soprano solo as Miss Pincher intensely active at piano.

A rustling in the wings behind the folding screen. Mary and Joseph visible now, approaching Inn. Mothers go 'Oooh!' and 'Aaah!'

Teddy has his arm round Pippa's waist, so sweet. The Inn door opens wide. Will Aaron keep his promise? And be nice?

Apparently he will. He has a big grin on his face today.

'*Welcome!*' shouts the friendly, caring Innkeeper, throwing out his arms, no doubt a gesture learnt from mother's little drama group. 'Welcome, and come inside!'

He pauses, then piles on the welcome.

'*We bloody got plenty of fucking room today!*'

'Know what I'd really like for Christmas?' he said,

144

dithering about in kitchen doorway Sat. morning, after breakfast, pyjamas unbuttoned showing chest hair and God knows what else besides.

'Cover yourself up,' I said.

'A good old knees-up, that's what,' he replied.

He went to get his clothes on. I don't know what I thought he was going to say; fresh young bimbo with long, chunky thighs, maybe; enormous legacy, packet of lettuce seed perhaps. But when he'd gone I looked at cereal bowls that I was washing up and thought, He's right.

That's what was needed now the fun and games at school was over; my daughter most and then the baby and dear Wayne, my aunts Flo and Vi, who are Dad's sisters, Purkisses; their brother, the only living one, Uncle Eamonn, bit of a lush – no, what am I saying, I mean total inebriate, so stoned, usually at Christmas, he says, 'Merry Chrish . . . Chrish . . . Oh bugger it, I forget.'

And of course my dear Sister and her husband Roderick, who I should have married only I sent him a Dear John while he was off doing his National Service and I took up with Stan. And when he come back and noticed Amy, who was seventeen by then, I wanted him again and couldn't get him.

I got all sentimental going to look at book of telephone numbers and preparing to ring the lot.

Of course he had to come past and say, 'Ringing London? That'll cost a bomb. Send them all a post card, why don't you.'

I said, 'I haven't seen my only sister since September and you want me to send her a *post card*?'

'She can read, can't she?' he said.

When he'd gone I called Aunt Florrie, who was delighted to hear me and said, 'Oh good. Are we going to meet all your Norfolk friends?'

Well, that set me back a bit because of course, we haven't made too many. He says a lot of it my fault, I look down my nose and flash the London bit too much; everyone here *knows* they're in the provinces, for heaven's sake, you don't need to tell them – though I still maintain people should know their place, particularly provincials.

Poor Florrie wondering aloud if she got wardrobe suitable for Christmas in the country.

'Just come as you are,' I told her and she giggled and said she thought not – unless pair gent's dunga-rees acceptable, under pink nylong pinny because chilly serving in chocolate shop along with hair tied up in 'Forties turban and old sheepskin moccasins on feet.

'Auntie – whatever turns you on,' I say, and she screams with laughter.

Then I ask cautiously after Eamonn.

Silence. Then Vi's voice saying, 'Who is it?'

Flo: 'Shut up. I can't hear.'

Vi: 'No, but who is it?'

Flo: ''Reeny. Go away.'

Vi: 'Lemme talk to her.'

Flo: 'No. 'Reeny – you still there?'

And all the time I'm dreading Stanley coming back and finding me. Once more I try a careful question about Eamonn.

'He's fine,' Flo says after a little think. 'Just fine. You needn't worry about asking him for Christmas.'

Still puzzling whether this means don't ask him at any price or I should feel free to do so without a qualm when hear S. coming back so hang up suddenly, which must surprise her.

But he knows.

'Bloody hell, Mog – where we going to get the money?' he demands. 'And you ringing up and inviting everyone – how we going to feed them all, eh, eh? How we going to feed ourselves, for heaven's sake?'

'Something'll turn up.'

'Bloody better,' he growls. 'And you send pc's to all the rest, you hear me?'

'To hear is to obey, O Great One,' I say, and wait until he gone again, out to garage, and then quickly snatch up handset and dial Dorelia.

But she's got Wayne's perfect mother coming Christmas time.

D. says, 'Between you and me, Mum, she's rather a sad lady. You know Wayne's father died six months ago.'

Well, so I did. I sent the woman a nice tasteful card with CONDOLENCES written on it in big silver letters and a raised picture of two praying hands. She ought to have cheered up by now.

We've never met. During the wedding she in hospital with historectomy. Some large, mumsy, Coronation Street character I imagined her, all duster and rinsed milk bottles.

Well, Christmas and charity and all that. D. better bring her along too. Do her good to see how babies brought up in the Purkiss manner.

Went and told Stan.

He threw up hands in gesture of despair.

Takes a lot to make him throw his hands about.

I said, 'Anyone think you was Eyeti or Red Indian or summing. Don't be melodramatic. Thought you wanted Family.'

'Not if they got to sleep outside in the sodding road!'

He pottered off to greenhouse then to fix hardboard where a cracked pane used to be and a bright new fresh idea struck me and I called Dorelia again

147

and told her to bring lilo's, camp beds, sleeping bags
and anything else she could lay hands on and while
about it, to call her Auntie Amy and tell her to do
the same.

He come in as I finished – didn't hear me this
time – saying, 'ow about 'ammock in the garden for
one or two of them? Puzzle Eamonn, that 'ammock,
he said, laughing loudly at own joke as always,
even if he sober for a few days, which he won't
be. Not many of Purkiss relatives are at Christmas,
eh, eh, eh?

I said, 'That's enough about my relatives. At least
Purkisses know how to enjoy themselves, and don't
sit there like a death's head at the feast.'

He said, 'What you mean by that?'

'Never you mind,' I told him darkly and mysteri-
ous. 'But I saw you blubbing during the Queen's
speech last year.'

I picked a teatowel up and handed him the cereal
bowls from breakfast.

'I'm a monarchist,' he protested with a feeble
attempt at simple dignity. 'And at least I don't sit
there trying to get peanuts in my . . .'

'Just dry the plates,' I told him, and left him
standing there and went out to the garidge meself
to look at all the summer stuff stored there and
wonder if we could flash any of it around in
winter.

I traced a dust trail on the wheelie gas-bottle
barbie and thought, Last time I touched you I still
had lovemaking with Todd to come, and now I don't
know where he is, and no means of finding out,
neither, not without giving meself away.

Look at me, I thought. My age – and I only ever
had two men in all me life.

Nothing ever turns out as it ought.

Went back indoors again and put my arms round Stan. Well, I got stretchy arms.

I bought him B.B.C. *Gardener's World* diary for Christmas. Dunno what else to get him – life-size rubber dolly with specially inflatable thighs?

Brooding.

Nipped next door into Mavis for brown sugar and found she invited her daughter and family up Christmas Day and Boxing Day, then going down with them to Essex for rest of holiday. She then said, looking out at lowering sky, 'I think I'll close up for the afternoon. Me regulars mostly been in anyway.'

Made snack lunch, big pot of tea. Got on with bobble hats while he watched film.

Later, going up to bed, he all affectionate. Pretended it was Todd.

'Just like old times,' he said, chuckling, afterwards. 'You're my best girl, you know that?'

'First among many, eh?'

'You know I didn't mean that.'

'What you go off for, then?'

'I wish you wouldn't keep bringing that up!'

'I bet you do wish that an' all.'

'What you want?' he asked, all sudden. 'I never know.' He raised himself up on elbow and looked down, not that he could see, because the light was off.

'Moggy,' he said. 'Moggy – you got fancy man?'

'No, I ain't,' I said truthful. 'Why?'

'Mavis said . . .'

'What did Mavis say?'

'Said she saw you. With someone.'

'Oh.'

'You ain't denying it, then?'

'How can I when I don't know what Mavis saw?'

'Mavis never saw nothing,' he said, laying back. 'I just made it up.'

'What a lousy trick.'

'Yes, but you fell for it, didn't you?' he said, all triumphant. 'Now I know.'

He settled on his other side, turned over and withdrew his arm. When he'd gone I felt chilly, but I had a faint, glad feeling of having kicked him in the balls somehow. He'd gone off and I'd repaid him and he knew. Serve him right.

But it was chilly without his arm.

'How long's it been going on?' he asked.

'I told you, there's nothing,' I said, using, not meaning to, the same words he used to me about that tart.

'Don't gimme that. You had a different smell on you once or twice when you come in, it clung to that long, blond hair you're so proud of. Sweetish smell.'

'It's them cigarettes. Everyone uses them round here or haven't you noticed. Callum rolls 'em.'

'Oh, so it was Callum, was it?'

'Don't be bloody daft.'

'You admit there was someone, though?'

'No.'

I didn't say another word, just turned on my side, and after a short while, I slept.

The good feeling of having kicked him faded fast. In the small hours a cold wind got up from somewhere and began blowing quietly about the room and I woke up, all uneasy. Bet he didn't feel no cold draught on him, though.

Or maybe he did and he just didn't say.

You never saw winter like they got round here. I don't mean severe, you can go to blimming North

150

Pole or Derbyshire or somewhere for that, but dreary. Miles and miles of not-so-sweet FA, covered by miles and miles of damp grey cloud. That's when there's not frost or soaking rain. There's varieties of dreariness.

They ripped out most of the trees and hedges bordering the fields round here some years ago, prairie farming, they call it because farmers greedy. Well, I mean – I never saw a poor one, like you never see a poor solicitor.

And the wind . . .

I moaned to Callum in The Street about it and he said it was geography; country here stuck out into North Sea like bustle on old-fashioned dress.

'Or someone's big fat bum,' I added, and he said, 'Yeah – all fulla shits, eh?' – looking at me slyly with his eyes and laughing.

'Yew don't loik it, yew shouldna joined,' he said suddenly in broad Norfolk. 'Yew should've went home to Lon'on.'

They don't say the hard little sounds in words round here. Village called Letheringsett nearby he calls 'Larinset', and instead of Sheringham, he says 'Shernham'.

Stanley come into Mavis' shop to help me carry groceries later and when we got home he started into *'Ain't it a pity she's only one titty'* before he remembered he was still sulking from last night.

I don't think he's got any right to sulk. He started it.

Rice pudding twice this weekend.

Sunday. I think I'm gonna have to shelve this immortal prose for a bit. He's not just not speaking, he's ignoring me. So choked I can't hardly write.

Said to him, 'What's this 'orrible silence, then?'
(We always had summing to say even if only "I just
done those dishes, dummy!")

He said, 'I don't talk to tarts.'

'You bloody managed it for three whole months
this year!' I told him.

'That's different,' he informed me.

'Oh? You mind telling me *how* different?'

'She weren't my legal wedded wife.'

I was so surprised at him I couldn't think what
to say to him, and then, unable to resist it, told
him, 'She's someone else's now. And probably still
offering it around.'

He just stood and stared at me. I swear he went
white in the face.

'How do you know?' he whispered.

'And she's in the pudding club an' all. Amy
told me.'

'How far . . . I mean, how long . . .'

'Any minute now, I gather, and it'll be a monster.
Bitch like that couldn't possibly give birth to nor-
mal child.'

'Don't call her a bitch.'

'But she was, Stanley, she was!' I screamed. 'She
was the biggest fucking bitch I ever saw. Bitch!
Bitch! *Bitch!*'

'That's enough!' he said, turning away, but I yelled,
'Oh no it isn't, Stanley Spink, you bloody hypocrite!
You go around, having it off with whoever you please
and then you come home and say you're sorry, you
just been a naughty boy and get taken back without
a murmur, *without a* murmur, and I do it just the
twice and I get called all evil names and told I'm
a tart. Well if I'm a tart, what does that make *you*,
Stanley, shacking up like you did and still drooling
over it, and don't tell me you ain't! It isn't fair!'

'It's different for a woman,' my Stanley said.

'By God, I always thought you was thick, and now I know it, dragging archilogical stuff like that out! Women was only tarts when they had babies!'

'You called her one quick enough.'

'Yeah, well she's pregnant.'

Got him. He still very white in face.

'If ever I needed to know the Purkisses are common,' he said, 'I know it now.'

'At least my parents were married!'

'And what's that supposed to mean?'

'Exactly what it sounds like. You're a bastard.'

'Yeah? Well maybe I got baby bastard coming an' all.'

'Well maybe you'd better trot down there and see if they'll let it call you Daddy then, but if I was Scumbag's husband I wouldn't even let you in the door. I mean, he's really going to want to know you, isn't he – the chap who was knocking off his wife, his *legal wedded wife*.'

I won that set. I won whole round, really. He in wrong and knew it and only trotting out pompous old macho attitudes because he ain't got nothing else.

So now we have Cold War. God, he gets more and more like his bloody mother every day! Postulant and mean and spiteful and petty, petty, petty . . .

I had a pullover for him, but he won't get it now. It's blu to go with bobble hats and will suit me nicely. Also I got housecare manual for Wayne, all about plumbing, which he's bound to love, so I think I'll give him gardening diary and bobble hat as well.

Serve the bugger right!

*

153

Rain, rain, rain! Stair rods of it, drumming over fields. Blu fungus on the inside wall of garidge. Can't even get into Mavis' without getting bloody soaked.

Cold War deteeriating into grunts. Might as well be marroned on desert island with a pig for company. (Well?)

He determined to behave like wronged party still, and lets me see this by his gracious manner. Him and his ancient double standard. Sod that for a game of soldiers.

I got a tree in all the same from Mavis and decorated it and put his presents that I'm giving Wayne underneath it.

For Mrs Leech, his perfect mother who does everything about the house so well (no one else ever does, of course), I got a book of knitting patterns, none of your Vogue stuff, just your basic plain and purl, some warm but not too glamorous furry slippers – and a tasteful matching ovenglove-teatowel-plastic apron set, printed in cabbages with spring garden border, Littlewoods M.O.

(Lucky we got them divans from them before the Crash, also the rosewood pianette, not that I play, but Amy does and you gotta have somewhere to stand photographs of the baby.)

For my Dorelia I got set easy roast, oven-to-table ware in Royal Worcester, craftsman-made, real porcelain, 'Evesham Vale' design. Now I worried this won't balance with Wayne's presents, he getting Stanley's lot and all.

For baby Jane I got big rocking horse, and for Aunties I got sexy nighties (tact), also perfume, well, cologne. And I put miniature whisky bottle in Vi's parcel and tube of Smarties in Flo's.

Things looking good all round house even if we

do have to take out second mortgage to pay for everyone's food.

Lovely scent of pine branches, lavender wax polish, apples, oranges and wood smoke. Said to him not to forget to pick Vi and Florrie up down the station tomorrow morning, they coming Christmas Eve Eve, and he said fat chance of forgetting.

I said, 'For Gawd's sake behave cheerful!' And he said, 'Why?' And I just looked at him, and he said, 'Oh, alright.'

Thank God we ain't got Countess coming this year, that's all I can say – unless she walks from Crystal Palace Cemetery where she's in her grave and her bum's cold and the whole whiskery, massive length of her as well, I shouldn't wonder.

He got ivy from the wild part of the garden and twinned it everywhere, also paper chains and dingly-dangly things. And I got nice red paper serviettes from Mavis and while in there thought that as so many coming this year would also buy paper tablecloths to save on laundry. So got two or three of those as well, tastefully decorated round edge with seasonal fat Father Christmases and holly.

I done two puddings and bought one in case it needed, also large cake and iced it, also Dundee and chocolate log and sponge and worrying now the plump and perfect Mrs Leech will think they're not up to standard. Still, if she's like her son at all she's bound to be a nice body. And who cares if she's fat? I got secret plans to stand next to her and look quite slim.

Darren would have been thirty years old today.

Sent him off to get Aunties while made pot of tea. Then they at door, all emotional and tearful, the dears, Auntie Vi with skinny arms wide for hugging and A. Florrie lumbering and panting up there behind her, larger than ever this year.

Both exclaiming over beautiful new house and for a minute I see it all fresh through their eyes and not lovely, hated lonely place it is at times. All set to give them guided tour except Stanley wanting tea and Aunt Vi whispering to me for summing a bit stronger.

No squabbling over the best bed this year, they both got the Littlewoods' divans we bought before the Crash.

Dorelia's old bed in other spare room for Wayne's mother. Popped my head in to check that all decent for the poor grieving, homely soul; Victorian-style wash stand and towel with attractive jacquard satin applique rose pattern, fully absorbent, machine-washable, fluffy towels and their matching pink foot mat with nonslip latex backing.

Looked round very satisfied and thought she must be hard to please indeed if she didn't appreciate all this. He'd even put sprigs of holly and ivy up here behind the tasteful coloured prints I got of Victorian kiddies in their nightgowns, also them cute little dogs begging for biscuits with appropriate sentimental captions. I even got Gramma Purkiss' old straw hat and veil she wore when making poteen in little brick built outhouse, Tralee, County Kerry, circa 1895, when Grandpa come courting with a horse and cart and banjo, but that, as we authors say, another story.

Enough to send anyone to sleep, this room.

Mind, the queen-posts in the far wall — I think I heard S. say they hold the rafters up — do somehow contradict my lovely things. They look all stern and sort of reproving at the hat and veil so very strong and black against the doodahs. Perhaps S. can paint them over sometime.

White, I think. You'd hardly notice them then.

Downstairs, now, to where Aunt Vi making inroads into sherry and Aunt Flo kicking off new shoes under the settee.

Ask cautiously for news, show baby photographs, explain Roderick and Amy coming later.

Pause.

Then dive right in and ask if Uncle Eamonn still shacking up with dirty Irish tart from Feathers, the one who keeps kitchen surfaces so you stick to them.

Aunties look at one another and seem about to say summing when thump, thump at the back door and Callum's voice calling out about alright for drinks on Christmas Eve?

Go out to ask him in but he refuses. Go back and tell Aunties who that was and what he wanted.

'A cocktail party?' Auntie Vi says, perking up, and Florrie wonders doubtfully what she should wear.

'Nice, though,' she says chattily. 'Funny, in your letters you made them sound backward and not too friendly, summow.'

Christmas Eve. Sent S. down the town for more sherry, A. Vi apparently developing hollow legs. Though not, I must record in all fairness, as bad as brother Eamonn for the stuff, she thinks it comes out of taps at Christmas time.

Also Easter, Bank holidays and summer months in Teneriffe, but that too another story.

Flo goes off with Stanley to get a glimpse of the sea but Vi stays with me and the bottles and tells of Christmases so hard they had no presents and only a few sausages for dinner. She recalls being sent to

157

grocer's to buy ha'penny worth of broken biscuits for a treat and I say surely worf another sherry, that one, Auntie, and she brightens.

So Vi gets tiddly? She's my auntie, and she got Purkiss blood. Drink up, I say – it's Christmas. I'll join her in a minute. And she giggles and wonders did we ought, it's only two o'clock. But that just for form's sake. I know and she knows, and she knows I know and I know she knows I know she must make a little pretence, though only God knows why. Comes from the Purkisses being upwardly mobile, I suppose.

Round to Callum's railway carriage later, Aunties all poshed up and eager to nose inside; Flo in new shoes and Vi all hideous in dark red lipstick. Knock and stand and wait in moaning wind only to find Callum and father out, or at least not answering railway carriage door.

Squelch back down the unmade lane with Aunties hugely disappointed, saying can't understand it, must be a mistake (it is; Callum meant see the whole lot of us in pub) and go back soaked – though not precisely in the way that Auntie Vi had hoped.

However, S. got huge fire going, must've put on whole tree, and now puts out brandy and little glass dishes full of nuts and cheesey things, and pulls chairs up and draws my cosy, rosy curtains. Vi and Flo shiver with sensations; this is what they understood by Christmas in the country – and Stan pours Vi extra large brandy, all medicinal, gotta keep the damp from reaching the bones.

Laying tea, when Dorelia, baby, Wayne and perfect Mrs Leech arrive, only – 'orrid shock, she ain't plump at all, but tall and elegant with crisp silver hair, red lips, and beautifully made up eyes with blu mascara. Blu velvet jacket, long silk skirt and shiny dark blu boots with little tassels that go swish-swish as she walks. Anything further from Old Mother Home-cooked Dumplings hard to imagine.

I reel back, then hug Dorelia, baby, Wayne, from habit, then kiss air three inches from Mrs Leech's powdered cheek, since she offers, feeling very fat and shiny faced. She smells expensive and delicious. Nothing much Littlewood's with her.

Still reeling, heart in boots. Remember Auntie Vi at stage now when ready to do things with peanuts. Hell. Also Flo will have cast off her shoes.

Wayne, who has driven the little party up, asks if alright to park in drive and Stanley nods. He then does honours with drinks and baby Janie cries because fed up and then I take Mrs Leech upstairs to show off house and indicate the Little Mermaids' Room.

'Oh, not "Mrs Leech", *Leila, please*,' she says, and I say 'Fine, I'm 'Reen.'

She smiles and says, 'I've been looking forward to meeting you, Irene.'

Hell.

'And we're both grandmammas!' I say.

She rolls her eyes to heaven and gives little groan.

She's older than me by about ten years but doesn't look it. Tells me she's a receptionist for this plastics company down St Mary Cray. All I can say is they're not making receptionists like they used; this one all groomed, poised like that Barbara Goalen in the 'Fifties. And she got smooth, haughtycultural voice like old Ma Thatcher.

Just comforting self that cottage at least up to standard when two thoughts strike home; if she works in St Mary Cray, it's likely she knows Vi's and Florrie's little corner shop. Also the presents! What's she going to make of ovenglove and teatowel set, for heaven's sake?

Hell.

She probably got dishwasher and has a woman in twice a week to do the rough.

And as if this not bad enough, later I see her running a finger along shelf over ingle nook when she thinks no one's looking and making grimace about what she found.

Yes, yes, I know – six months ago I would have thought the same. Now I long to tell her always dust in country houses where you got open fire, especially one as big as this, even if you just dusted. But I can't.

Baby Jane crawling. Everyone makes noises, even Auntie Vi, who has been separated from the peanuts. It's evident that baby got strong dose of Purkiss genes when her mother removes a set of fire irons that little Janie particularly wanted, and she speaks her mind.

'Fine pair of lungs on her,' Stanley observes to Mrs Perfect, who can't deny.

She down for a little nap on the settee then and I dish up. Sit to table and watch Florrie gobbling, Stan getting into cutlet and feel nervous. Are the peas small and green enough, I wonder, worrying again about the pressies and offering silent prayer of thanks that Eamonn at least far away in London and not bringing full compliment of red, red Purkiss blood to parade in front of Leila.

I see her shoot a look or two at Aunties then, and think, What the hell! So they hold their knives and forks like chopsticks? They don't prune and prism over food, thing I can't stand, taking little piece of potato and one pea on a fork prong, singly. Our family all shovel like Prince Charles; he had his mummy's permission to do it, so I'm told.

All well on surface, though. I play the 'ostess. Done a special treacle tart. Tasteful, seasonal tapes in background like posh restaurants though personally, voice of Cliff Richard makes me want to vomit.

'Oh, but he does such a lot for charity,' the perfect Leila smiles.

'Does little for my eardrums,' I retort, but she just smiles again all sweet and supersillyous.

Stan come in sharp at this point laughing and saying, 'Carol singers! Quick, lie down on the floor, everyone!' And then he adds any more 'ipocrytes come round, they get thick 'ear instead of ten pence, we got enough already with the mother of local child abuser going round proffering parish magazines. Would have kissed him but remembered we not speaking.

Thought perhaps Perfect might loosen up a bit once she got food and wine inside her, but no. When all drawing chairs up to fire and pushing parcels surreptitios on to pile by tree and preparing to have nuts and brandy, she enquiring if a church round here and if so, is there Midnight Mass? And about eleven she sets off across the fields taking Wayne and Stan's best flashlight with her, one of them not too sober and not arguing.

S., with a few drinks on board, forgot and said to me he'd like to stick a pin in her and see if he draw blu blood to match her jacket, and then remembered that his wife a tart and drew back smartly.

D. filming little Jane by tree, holding up her hands for parcels. Vi says, 'Let's have a drink. It is Christmas, after all.' And I ask D. if she sees much of Leila and get answer more than they did when

161

she lived up in Essex, but she wouldn't dream of just dropping in – always telephones first to make sure it convenient.

All sitting round fire baking shins when they come in, the religious one and her child, who is sober now and ratty. Stan rolls sleeping Auntie Flo in her flowered armchair away on its castors so Leila can come to fire and pours Wayne brandy.

'Oh, I don't think he'll want that,' Leila says. 'He just told me he was going to bed.'

Wayne says he changed his mind.

Soon after Leila went up to sleep with the forbidding queen-posts and Auntie Flo woke up, mumbling about being far away from fire. Wayne wheeled her back and did a brandy round. I saw Vi had snuck the peanuts back but it didn't matter now. The flames roared on. Fatgirl come in, wild to be let out to slaughter things.

When we went up I whispered to Stanley, 'Four whole days!' – forgetting the Cold War. He just said tersely, 'Shut your eyes and be as civil as you would to that fancy man of yours!'

We was in bed with the light out and I lay there hoping he'd turn over and we sleep spoons but no. I thought, Sod you, and was awake some time wondering if that Leila ever excited over anything and if she got steamed up over Mr Perfect when he was alive.

Then I thought, Be kind, she's recently bereaved, and made plans to talk to her and do things like showing her the gnomes tomorrow. Fell asleep.

She didn't sneer at the gnomes outright, she was too busy getting out party manners on parade, making sure they snapped to it and were polished, but I could see she thought gnomes common,

162

especially the ones with little fishing rods.

I think she thinks Stanley common too (well, he is), and that Wayne married beneath himself and little Janie some sort of half-breed, therefore.

Miserable.

Couldn't say nothing, of course. But I come on her staring in wonderment at all me brass bits everywhere, and she never said a word about the beautiful bedroom she had, as I thought she might. I got feeling she was sneering inside herself at everything; well it may have been her tummy rumbling, but I doubt it.

Still, we got to make her welcome, so I went right on, stopping Stanley singing in the bath before he started and keeping Vi and the sherry bottle tucked away. Might seem as if it easier to keep Vi and sherry bottle apart but no; they joined at the wrist just like those twins and sooner or later the peanuts in evidence too. Next Christmas there'll be total exclusion of peanuts.

Or will there? Trouble with Christmas is always too much, too soon, too many people all crammed together in few little days, no wonder emotions bubble over. And that's why Auntie like she is at Christmas, keeping wide smile on her face as she commits excesses; you gotta be happy and jolly no matter how much you longing to bang people's heads together or how much your dogs are barking.

So I rush about, keeping place neatish and seeing everyone got food and drink and contented – and thinking to myself, inside, Only three more days.

Roderick and my dear Sister turn up Christmas morning, with the mongrol she rescued from being ill-treated in Sevenoaks twelve months ago. He'd grown a bit but not much and when Fatgirl saw him she just looked at him and dared him to come closer. Fella put his tail between his legs.

Perfect Leila said, 'How sweet!' and I knew why. Your Royal Family has dogs. Cats is common. She said she'd save a turkey bone for him special, sweet little doggie-thing, and Amy, bless her, said at once, noway; cooked bones might splinter in his throat.

Well then, coos perfect Leila, not put off, he shall have a walkie, and Amy says she don't think so, they stopped off on Norwich road so he could pee and he went off and had enough walkies for ten dogs and wouldn't come when called.

So then Leila says, still smiling, 'Come for a cuddle, poor little doggie!' And that's when Amy tells her Fella picked up fleas.

Shriek! And I have to turn away to hide me face. Amy upsets apple cart still further by tying Fella up in kitchen (I don't object) where fleas can hop about all insanitary.

That dog ain't really got fleas. I know my Sister, quick to size people up. I give her chocolate biscuit, hug, a cuppa tea, first cracker off the tree, glasser wine, mint After Eight and big wet kiss, and she looks at me all shaken, as she would be. She more used to 'Reeny hitting her, and always has been.

Then Roderick come in kitchen, bearing the Glenlivet, five bots, and I see perfect Leila over-awed by his black curling beard, his height, and triffic style as he pours malt whisky, tossing cork carelessly away where he won't find it with as fine an action as any of my Duke's. And I can see Leila noting that Roderick neither a Purkiss nor a Spink, and faintly puzzled.

I cheer up.

We all have a dram, and then another, even

Leila, and the atmospherics lighten. Only two more days!

Even old Ladida enjoyed my Christmas dinner, though Stanley come near to spoiling it with his 'Do have an intercourse cigarette if you want one, ho, ho, ho!' Longed to tell her that he meant well though he common, but I couldn't.

Then when the nuts and fruit and crackers over, what does he go and do but suggest we have a bit of a sing-song after dinner.

I looked round for help but there wasn't any, not even Amy, she stacking plates in kitchen. Mrs Perfect just went on smoking, lips curling in a smile. Then Stanley decides aloud that what we *really* need is a good old-fashioned knees-up, and thank goodness we still got Dorelia's guitar and the new pianette.

'We haven't had it long,' he confides to Leila confidentially. 'To be quite honest with you I thought it blimming waste of good money – there's none in this house can play the silly thing. But Amy's a clever girl, and she'll oblige.'

I could of died then, except I wanted to murder Stanley. I smiled across at Leila who didn't smile, and I threw a spoon at Stanley as if in play and it hit him on the nose and made his eyes water, and I was glad.

He went out to kitchen, carrying pile of pudding plates to Amy and I followed after, forgetting the Cold War.

'You little *sod!*' I hissed. 'Bring out the brown ale, why don't you? Get cockles, whelks and jellied eels! Let's have some fish and chips in paper bags or better still, wrapped in *The Sun* or *Daily Mirror*, eh?

He just looked back at me all surprised – I think

165

he'd forgotten we weren't speaking, too – eyes big and wary and said he just had dinner, thanks, and wasn't hungry.

Wayne laughing now and D. giggling the way she often does and cannot stop. The Aunts watching, puzzled, specially Vi. Oh, what the Hell.

So we had the old songs, couldn't help it, because my dear Sister went to pianette and began to play. We had *My old man*, *The Lambeth Walk*, *Knees up, Mother Brown!*, progressing to *The Foggy, Foggy Dew*. Should just be thankful she don't know *Balls to Mr Bangelstein*, I thought as I went to sort out kitchen.

After a bit the music stopped and there was a noise of talking in the sitting room. I got on with me saucepans, feeling sorry for myself, and then the piano started up again. Seemed to be a game, this time, making up a song with everybody contributing different lines.

I drew deep breath. We're alright here, I thought. Leila will see we're not just a bunch of thicko's. Our family quite good at rhymes.

But I'd reckoned without that Stanley.

A little way down the road from us in Norwood, well out on the Sevenoaks Road to be exact, was a caravan company, sold caravans, wouldn't you know, name of *Gailey Caravans*, tickled our Stanley a lot. Well, he easily amused.

'Silly name,' he'd say, to which I'd retort, 'No sillier than Spink.'

Now he was obviously remembering the name *Gailey*.

'Gailey, Gailey!' (came his voice) '*Likes it daily . . .*'

'*With a choirboy or two.*' (Wayne's voice.)

Oh no!

Then Wayne's voice again, correcting: 'Make that four.'

Amy began the musical phrase again, some old 'ymn tune, and they started over.

'Gailey, Gailey, likes it daily
With a choirboy or four . . .'
'But the curate can't endure it – ' (Amy?)
''Cause it makes his plonker sore! (Stan)
  But the rector, a perfector of the cunning anal
ploy . . .' (Unidentified female voice, but I fear, I
very much fear that's my Dorelia)
'Vaselines his little penis' (Roderick?)
'And his pleasure's unalloyed!' (Mrs Perfect Leila
Leech?)

Shouts of laughter. I can hear Flo's cackle clear
above the rest. Are they all *blind drunk*? Then
Amy's voice: 'Not bad. Now, all together!' And
they go into song again, the Aunties too. I am
horrified. Roderick must have been too liberal with
the Glenlivet. I drop saucepans and charge in.

Mrs Perfect wiping tears of blu mascara, Roderick
doubled up, Aunt Flo wheezing and trying to get
breath, Dorelia nearly wetting self, and as for
Stanley . . .

How does she do it, bloody sister Amy? How does
she do it? That's what I want to know.

Boxing Day afternoon, Wayne tells me all casual
his mother is an undeveloped intellectual and is
thinking of applying for an Open University degree
course in Eng. Lit.

'Oh, did you tell her I write poetry?' I cried.

'Er – no.'

'Why not, if she's all intellectual? Unless you
think my poetry's not good enough?'

'Oh no!'

'No you do think that or no you just didn't tell her?'

'Neither. It's just I . . .'

I looked at him suspicious. 'I written romantic novel,' I told him, forgetting that he'd seen some of the pages.

'Well when I say I written, what I mean is, several chapters,' I told him. 'Well, that is, a chunk. A bit. Well, I started it. I remember now, you saw it. You said to me, "Outline your plot."'

'I did?'

'Yeah. You remember. You said, "A perfect pastiche or summing." You remember. And you said to put raw sex in.'

His face cleared in memory. Then it clouded over again.

'Not got it about the house, have you?'

'Oh yes!' I said, getting all excited, thinking he wanted to show it to his mother. 'In the buro drawer. I'll get it, shall I?'

'No. Yes.'

'Make up your mind.'

'There's little Janie crying,' he said suddenly. 'Why doesn't Do go up to her?'

'It's all the intellectual noise in there,' I said. 'Probably can't hear.'

Well, I may have been wrong, but I thought he was fighting a bit shy of looking at THE DUKE, and being very sensitive about it, I let it go. I went up to little Janie and played with her and she was glad to see me and laughed and played and wet herself and generally showed what a clever child she was.

In an intellectual way, of course. Oh yes.

We both went down after a bit and into the kitchen to make 'am sandwiches. Then we took

168

them and the chocolate log into the sitting room where all the intellect was. You never seen 'am sandwiches disappear so fast.

That Leila had unbent at last and was chatting to Amy about life in plastic, the Aunties were still playing with their presents like small children.

(All the awkwardness over those resolved alright; I just altered labels and gave Flo's to Leila, dunno what she made of the Smarties. Flo never know the difference now. And I give Stanley his bobble hat and things to show no ill feeling. The bobble wobbles when he moves his head and when Dorelia first saw that I thought she'd die. She laughed so much her eyes were streaming tears.)

Well, still nobody asked me to open buro drawer, take DUKE out and read, and I was beginning to work on remarks that might lead them up to it, when there was a heavy knock at the front door.

And oh my God it was either Eamonn Purkiss there or his twin brother. And holding him by the hand was squarest, most doggo bird I have ever seen.

I don't think I ever see Eamonn sober in all me life. I can't remember even seeing him walk straight – ever. Dad – he was the eldest of five, three girls (if you count Auntie Beat, she's dead), two boys – used to say Eamonn killing himself with the drink and now here he was on the doorstep and Dad, who never touched the stuff, dead more than thirty years.

I heard alcohol preserves. Or maybe our Eamonn just got a charmed life. Flo tells how he was a mechanic in the Fleet Air Arm during the last War and once walked smack into the turning propeller of a Swordfish he didn't particularly happen to see.

This accident accounted for what happened to his brains, Flo says. And that was before he let the sauce get to 'em.

Natty dresser, though; hair always slicked down and sideways, face cleanshaven even if the heavy creases of it looked as if holding dirt.

Now to my astonishment he smiled. I thought maybe I turning into pint of Guiness or summing and looked round.

''Ullo, 'Reeny, love!' he shouted and held out his arms.

He didn't smell of beer. He didn't smell of spirits. He smelt of aftershave and deodorant and everything else that's beautiful.

'You was expecting us, wasn't you?' he said, lovely big smile again. And I was so taken aback I opened my mouth and not a single word come out.

'Ahem!' said the big dog at his side.

'Oh, this here is Morag,' Uncle said proudly. 'The young lady.'

He might have said Queen Boadicea come back, I was so surprised. I mean he was married once, Auntie Shirl, we don't talk about her much, and he had that slattern up The Feathers, but this one looked butch – and very clean and sober.

Blimey, you needed a wide angle lens with her. She went on for miles, and would have been a tight fit in a National Park. And I thought I had weight problems!

She had 'ard face too, nothing smiling about her. She was all square-cut and chunky, tiny eyes and hair shaved up the sides and back, to show her tiny round gold studs permanent in her ears, I suppose. Forget what she was wearing, summing dung-coloured and unfestive. Maybe she just spent month of Methodist Sundays in that place dissembling Russians go. That would account for her — and not offering to shake hands or kiss or nothing.

They come in. I got the door open just in time or she would have gone through like a tank, leaving hole the shape of her, like Tom and Jerry.

Loadsa silence as we entered lounge. I'm sure I saw the spider plants recoil. I thought waspish, This a test for Amy. Let's see her get round Morag, eh?

The men stood up all civil, though Stanley a bit wobbly. Amy kissed her, Roderick offered the Glenlivet, as she another Scot, and everyone had some, even Auntie Vi, who to my certain knowledge laden well above the Plimsoll line already. I went to see about some tea, and when I come back there she was, all large on the settee and everyone else looking as if squeezed into rest of room.

Did them nice high tea with sardines and bacon rolls and devilled eggs, trifle, cheese and pickles, sponge with double cream, put Dorelia in my place at the table and Wayne in charge of drinkies and nipped next door to Mavis, hoping to catch her before she went down south. Wanted to borrow any camp beds she not needing on the journey.

I was 'alf hour in with her, still marvelling at Eamonn sober and when I come out it was snowing. Wayne said snow merited a brandy round and everyone laughed and said, 'It's snowing!'

Yeah, fancy that. Funny thing to happen in the British Isles in winter.

The men went into Mavis' to get the beds and came back saying she not going with her family; not too well and having a lay down. I envied her. Sent S. back with invitation to join us tomorrow, if she felt like it, then got on with washing up.

Made up camp beds on landing for us, having given Eamonn and the young lady our room. Dunno what they'll do in there, she don't look capable of passion.

Last snifters. Made sure kids comfortable in dining room, Amy and Roderick in lounge-sitting room. Use of bathroom in long relays. Tidied kitchen, set alarm — got to be up early to lay fires, make tea for all.

He grumbling mightily about alarm.

'Bloody lot of work, Christmas.'

'It is for some,' I said.

Hitting him, though I longed to do it, too intimate for when not speaking.

Flickering, peculiar white light trying to come in through chinks in landing curtains and alarm clock beside me on the floor clearing its throat, ready to go into act. Smack it on the nose.

Struggle up and out of camp bed. Long, happy, solitary cup of tea in kitchen. Turn Fella out remorseless into snow to piddle. Discover Amy up and doing fires.

Mavis in later saying she had physic foreknowledge this would happen, meaning thick snow, then added — we were alone in kitchen at the time — 'I see a broken wedding ring above your head.' And of course, I looked up. Silly.

She sees cymbals, being gifted that way in the air, and they show her what going to happen. I a little shaken because only a fool could mistake what a broken wedding ring might mean.

Stared at this nice, pink, homely body who could be everybody's auntie and said, 'Do you?'

She said summing to effect that if future known it can be avoided.

'You saying it won't happen, then?' I asked, but she was enematic. 'Not saying it will, not saying it won't. "The fault, dear Brutus, is not in our stars, but in ourselves that we are underlings."'

'Is that so?' I said, impressed. She had way of putting things.

Even Morag's pudden face changed when she saw the snow. Roderick called out, 'All hands to dig and shovel!' – and most went out, even that Leila, which I thought sporting.

Amy come with teatowel to do breakfast dishes and said, 'Maybe it'll thaw before too long.'

If it don't I got – I dunno how many days more with houseful of people instead of two.

Cold lunch. Glenlivet. Wayne asking if Mavis' Post Office and Stores also an off-licence, and being told it was, saying, 'A tunnel should be dug to it. Must keep vital lines of communication clear. Someone might want to post a letter.'

Strikes me young Jane stands to inherit boozy genes from both sides of her family.

More to the point, Mavis got huge freezer stocked full of frozen meat and veg and ready meals, also things like flour and powdered milk – but I doubt that Wayne or anyone else except Amy has thought of that bit yet.

Snow getting heavier. (Dec. 27th.) Very, very dark.

Made another trifle with the last of the sherry – sorry, Vi.

A good hot gammon supper. Then telephone went dead.

'Fault of all that ruddy *knitting*.' He incense, gold and myrrh, pointing up towards the ceiling.

173

'I *told* the bloke from Eastern Electric. Put it all underground, I said. Down south, I said, *we got it* underground, none of this overhead business, great poles everywhere. It wouldn't do in London, I told him.'

'What did he say?' Wayne asked with interest.

'Yes, well,' Stan said.

'You got ordinary white candles, Porky kid?' R. then enquired.

'Oh no!' I said. 'They wouldn't! Not at Christmas! They wouldn't cut it off, not at Christmas!'

'I don't think they got the weather properly under control yet,' Roderick said.

So I got the candles and stuck them round the rooms in saucers. I wouldn't let Roderick use my brass repro candlesticks with drip tray, finger holes, and little pointy-hat snuffers attached by tiny chains, and he was a mite irritated, I thought. Still maybe he physic like me and Mavis, for about ten o'clock, all the power went off.

S. had had the TV on, hoping for rerun of old Palladium programme with Tiller Girls and found *Five Thousand Years of the Two Ronnies* instead, didn't improve his temper.

'There were Ronnies before Christ,' I heard Wayne telling him, and Stanley starting to say, 'Get away . . .' when there we were in the dark, and just the light of the fire.

'Told you,' Uncle Eamonn said, though he'd done nothing of the sort. D. went to fetch the baby. Perfect Leila started looking round for cigarettes, and Stan said, 'Have a suck on my old pipe, duck, if you like.'

Well, what with dark and gamblers among us forming group for rummy and wondering if I could boil a kettle on the fire for some tea, I didn't notice

174

Stan at buro drawer. Next indication that he up to summing come when Eamonn asked, while dealing, 'What you got there, Stanley boy?'

'Summing 'Reen wrote,' S. said, not looking up from where he was holding DUKE to candle flame or two and no doubt searching for the dirty bits.

'What is it, recipes?' Flo asked.

'Never!' said Eamonn, squinting at his cards. 'HOW I GOT STANLEY TO THE ALTAR IN 'FIFTY-NINE, innit, cock?'

'Nothing like that,' Stanley said, grinning and shaking his head.

'Read us a bit,' Auntie Vi invited.

'Don't you dare!' I warned him in a whisper, though I was secretly rather pleased. I could see emergent-intellectual Leila listening with both ears.

'"'As I live,' vouchsafed the Duke,'" our Stanley read (from the chapter *In Which Our Heroine Is Excessively Dismayed*) '"'I am devilish pleased with this morning's work, egad.' He shot out a white and steely hand, marvellously embroidered at the cuff to reveal a priceless enamelled snuff box in the palm.

'"'My lady was prodigious lovely and she bobbed a curtsey, raising two great . . . pansy-brown eyes which were at once both dreamy and impish and shook a ringlet free from powder at him. One tiny hand toyed with a sweetmeat, the other caressed her pet monkey in the folds of her silken gown, while with the other hand she raised her quizzing glass. Her laugh was a ripple of water, quick and sure like a stream or a running brook or a mountain rill or a water spout or something.

'"'I beseech you, madam,' he said in tones which shook, telling of an innate, immense, overwhelming, blinding passion as he shot her a keen glance.

175

Then his sleepy, heavy, indolent, lazy white lids came down. 'I do beseech you – how may I serve you?'

""Oh, fie!' Evelina retorted, mentally consigning him to perdition and entertaining many an inadvertent animadversion on his admirable probity. A fan was spread. He saw her two great . . .""'

But here, rotten, lousy Stanley dropped the book and fell over in his chair, crying with helpless laughter, heaving and trying to get his breath. I could see Leila smiling, Wayne turning away his head. In a flash I'd leaped across the room and picked up the book. Can't remember if I said anything, but I do know I was crying.

Too upset to hit him properly I just whanged him round the ear and then hurled it in the buro drawer and slammed it shut.

'You 'orrible little prick!' I yelled at Stanley, not caring if the baby heard or not. 'You nasty, perverted, crumblin' little *fat* old fart! You twat, you bugger, you c . . .'

And then, well, summing made me stop. Maybe it was the sight of Dorelia's stricken face. I didn't dare look at that Leila or even Morag. They was all ganging up, I felt, wanting to laugh at me book and not one of them on my side.

Anyway, words not enough to say what I felt. What that Stanley needed was stuffing with the rough end of a pineapple and I was just about to run out of the room with the idea of finding one when summing very strange happened.

Pudden Morag suddenly got to her feet and shrieked out, 'I don't care what the rest of you say, I thought it was beautiful, just beautiful! Made me want to cry, it was so good. I fink it was sheer poetry!'

Too much Glenlivet, I thought. But she kept on.

'I don't know why you're laughing, all of you. You ought to be proud of her instead of laughing, proud she got education enough to write lovely stuff like that! If you'd been last of six brought up in a Glasgow slum, you'd know how to appreciate it instead of laughing!'

She sat down, rather flushed and looking round the room. I could tell that she was sober, well, certainly not pickled, just relaxed enough to say exactly what she thought. I nearly went and kissed her, specially when I see Eamonn nodding seriously, agreeing with every word she said.

I still didn't dare look at that Leila.

'Nobody's laughing,' Amy said, wiping her eyes, 'And if they tried it, they'd have me to deal with first.' Which seemed to set them all off again, those that were disposed to laugh.

'Oh, let's have a drink!' Wayne said, and went round with the brandy.

'Did you really write that, 'Reeny?' Flo come up and whisper. 'I thought it was very nice.'

Wayne did another round and just as he finished, two of the candles on the pianette went out with little pops.

'Stsk!' Stanley said, irritable and got up and put another log on fire. It didn't blaze up all at once and in the lull you could hear the moaning of the wind outside.

Then Mavis, who till now had been sitting very still and quiet in a corner, said, 'There's a presence in this room.'

Everyone looked over except Janie, who was playing with her toes, and Fatgirl, who was sleeping in a ball beside her. Fella, who'd been trying to get in with them both and who give up when I strode across the room, lifted his head.

'Mavis is a medium,' I said, for those that didn't know.

A bit of embarrassment, then, from those who evidently didn't believe, like Wayne and Morag. Maybe she one of the Wee Frees or summing, I thought. But Flo looked up all fearful and Vi and Roderick and Amy all stared where Mavis busy gazing, somewhere in the middle distance over Stanley Spink's right shoulder.

'Someone from time past,' that Mavis said, all deep and sepulchral.

'Oh, yes?' Eamonn said, as if she just introduced a neighbour, but I noticed he dropped his hand of cards and took a great swig at his orange juice.

And then all the lights went out; every single candle in the room snuffed itself and stood smoking, while the flames in the fireplace seemed to burn down low.

Vi screamed. Amy said, 'Give me your lighter, Uncle, or Leila – anyone! That's it. There's a draught in here.' And she stood up and tried to light the candles . . .

. . . but they wouldn't for some reason.

Mavis said, 'Leave it. He just wants firelight,' and I felt cold all down me spine.

'The dog! Look at the dog!' Vi cried out, pointing – and there was Fella, cringing against the settee and trying to dig through carpet to escape. Amy walked over and opened the door wide and Fella shot out, whining. But Fatgirl never even stirred.

'Who is it, dear?' Flo asked. Well, I think she knows the drill; goes once a week to meeting in little wooden hut in Sidcup, where everyone calls everyone else 'dear', and speakers tell you them in the spirit world saying all will be well when lilacs bloom again and Greataunt Alice sending message to say she watching with great interest and she *knows*.

'A man,' Mavis said in her dark voice. 'He's tall and fair. Wears a blue striped suit and brown suede shoes and looks a little like my friend here.' She indicated me. 'In fact he looks a lot like 'Reen, now he turns his head.'

I heard Eamonn give a groan, and I looked round. The man was quivering, the folded creases in his face and neck shaking like jelly.

'He's holding something up,' Mavis went on. 'It's — yes, I think it's a sort of microscope, very old and heavy-looking. Cumbersome. And now he's speaking, saying something about a little green statue. Jade, was it? At any rate, he was fond of it.'

'Oh, mercy!' Eamonn cried, spilling orange juice right across the table.

'Sean! I meant to get 'em back, I really did, but time run out and there wasn't faloose enough to redeem them! Say you forgive your little brother and understand! I'll make it up to Vi and Florrie and the girls. Say you forgive and understand!'

I never see such exhibition. We was all staring, amazed, especially that Leila, for now she weren't bored any longer, I could tell that. Eamonn stopped speaking, but now he was crying and he kept giving Mavis strange glances and holding up his hands as if to ward off a blow.

'Ye bludy fule!' come Morag's voice, all cutting and Scotch like Roderick's when he found me adding Diet Cola to the Glenlivet. 'Don't be so effing superstitious! There's nothing and there's nobody there!'

Personally, I didn't feel that I would bet on that. I couldn't see nothing, but I could sense *something* different in the room, and it felt like a Purkiss, laughing.

179

Dad, if it was him, was enjoying Eamonn being sorry.

The feeling of someone standing there laughing faded and I looked across at Eamonn and felt really sad for him because Morag was also looking at him, all contemptible, and I thought, there's one relationship just gone up the spout if he don't do summing pretty toot damn sweet.

And I was right.

'Who else is present, dear?' Flo asked, continuing form of service.

'A tall woman, got southern Irish brogue, saying she likes 'em big and broad, with hair so dark it got blu-black lights in it,' Mavis said — and Vi and Flo sort of clutched each other and whispered, 'Mam!'

'I don't believe it,' Stanley muttered.

The fire was burning right down. Nobody got up to see to it, though. The noise of the storm was increasing outside. Eamonn was still shaking like a jelly, thumbing through his pack of cards without seeing, and Morag, with an exclamation, got up and went over to the buro where she fished out THE DUKE, holding it up to me in the dim light as if to ask, 'May I?' I nodded.

'She's telling me you're coming into money,' Mavis went on. 'She's holding up some form of document — it may be a lease. You'll get your money's worth, she's saying. It's up to you, then, what you do with it.'

'Any tips, Mam?' Flo cried.

Mavis shook her head. 'Spirit doesn't concern itself with money.'

'When's it going to happen?' Vi asked, and Mavis shook her head again. 'Spirit doesn't concern itself with time.'

180

'Bloody should,' Stan said all low. 'If it really wanted to give 'and.'

Amy got up and succeeded in lighting the candles. Mrs Perfect lit a cigarette and sat smoking, amused at something. I wanted to kick her slim and beautifully covered shins. Well I ain't asking her for bloody Christmas again, that much is fixed and certain and for sure.

The candles filled the room with glowing radiance. People shifted positions, S. did the fire. Wayne went round with the brandy.

'Wait!' Mavis cried suddenly, and I thought, Oh God, what now? — forcing myself to be polite. 'There's another one, not been over too long, have you, sir? Name of Johnnie. And he's come with an apology.'

Well I could see most of us was pretty bored, except Eamonn, who was still a wreck. And Flo looked up hopeful, though she didn't know no one by name of Johnnie.

But that Leila did. You could tell by the way her eyes widened.

'He's sorry for . . .' Mavis began, then went on in aside, 'No, I won't say that, it's vulgar. You just change it.'

There was a pause. Leila stood frozen, waiting, though looking as if poised for flight.

'Oh, alright,' said Mavis to the unseen Johnnie. 'He's saying he wishes he hadn't bothered,' she said to Leila. 'Do you understand? I'm keeping part of it back because he's a gentleman who expresses himself forcibly.'

'Bitter, is he?' Flo put in, all chatty. 'You do sometimes get them bitter on the other side.'

Mavis and Leila ignored her. They looked at each other.

181

'I've a good mind to ring the police and have you arrested under the Fraudulent Mediums' Act,' Leila said softly.

'You'd have to prove that I was fraudulent, first,' Mavis replied, equally softly. 'Anyone seen any money change hands?'

But at that moment little Janie, who had been edging nearer and nearer to Fatgirl, created big diversion by poking a little finger in one of the cat's eyes. Fatgirl shrieked and leapt off the settee, complaining loudly, and Dorelia swooped on Janie, demanding the wild animal be removed, and Wayne thought he'd do a brandy round simultaneous with Roderick and the Glenlivet. (I mean, they disagreed about the drink.) Vi said, 'Both, please!' and held up two glasses, but Mavis, who'd probably had enough (of my family) thought she ought to be getting home.

Envied her, not for the first time, as she went to single bed in quiet, lonely house.

Thaw set in overnight.

Little Jane tried to stand today, only bright spot in it, and what does Eamonn do but encourage her, squatting down, holding out arms and saying all soppy, 'Come to Uncle-Wuncle, then!'

That Morag was scathing, saying don't he know it bad for their legs, trying to walk too soon, and he come back to ask what she know about such things, silly meddlin' old virgin? So I guessed they'd rowed and she hadn't let him have sex.

There was no further mention of the microscope or the little green jade statue.

It was thawing out fast by two o'clock, Morag rang the station taxi-rank and they said they thought they could get to her. So she went, and I was sorry in a way. She was the only one out of the nine who'd been pretty about the Duke.

Eamonn then said, 'Thank Christ she gone. I been dry too long – you know that? That preachin' ol' National 'Elf freak always trying to make me give up smoking. Now I can grow a beard and drink if I want to, pick me navel, fart in street. And she weren't givin' it away, for Chrisakes.'

I said, 'No?', all interested, but he wouldn't tell me more except to say she dangling her body at him for engagement ring.

'Poor old Uncle,' I said, sympathetic.

'Not so much of the old,' he urged. 'And poor? Not on your sweet life.'

And I think that just talk. I know he had a bit stashed away, but he must of drunk it all be now.

The older ones got round the fire in the afternoon, that Leila included. Roderick poured the Glenlivet for them (Wayne away outside, tunnelling through to Mavis and the shop) and they talked of Black Market trading in the last War and life in Bomb Alley; funny how talk always centres on the war at old ones' gatherings.

Eamonn told about tangling with that propeller, and Leila countered with a V2 in the back garden, and Vi said, 'You never? Right up your jacksie?' And they was all very merry with their doom and gloom.

Power come on some time in early morning. Amy got out hoover and helped me clean a bit.

'Lovely place,' she said to me, nodding at house.

'Lovely my backside,' I told her. 'It's not *Semper Idem.*'

She stared. 'But *Semper Idem* is you and Stan,' she said.

183

I sighed.

D. come in then with baby dressed in her little outing suit – they'd packed up while me and Amy cleaning. Now the Leeches ready to kiss and say goodbye and I felt wretched. I remembered how I'd envied that Mavis her empty house and wondered how I could.

Then that Leila come mincing down in her blu velvet to take her place in the family car and I knew just how. I didn't kick her shins, though, and I didn't say, 'Hope you topple off the twig toot sweet and get things straightened out with Johnnie.' A 'ostess has to wear a mask.

They drove off. Went back indoors, fed up to the eyeballs.

Vi was there, smiling and (nearly) sober. She'd polished all the glasses for me on a towel, and I ask you, what stronger sign could I have Christmas over? For I will say this for Vi, she knows when to draw the line and rest of the year she's dry, excluding festivals, as Methody Harvest Home.

Her brother made up for it, though. He ain't heard there is a line to draw. When I went back in the lounge there was Eamonn gaga on the last of the Glenlivet and clutching two bottles of tonic wine, one of gin and another of schnapps, which was all Wayne could find left in Mavis' store. By evening, Uncle was paralytic.

Same old thing always rolls round in time if you wait for it, I've found. (It was like that with flared trouser legs, which is why I've never altered some of mine, but kept them. Bell-bottoms will come in again, markey mes mots, tomorrow if not sooner.) So it was quite like old times when Stan and Roderick carried Eamonn to bed at end of evening, and I felt relief. Nice to know that some things never change, or only for a bit and then on course again, and Eamonn sober had disturbed me summow, as if sunflowers come up blu or moon square-shaped and only shining August.

That Stanley still not speaking, though; turning on right shoulder every night with never a hint of sleeping spoons. Not that I want to speak to him after his performance over THE DUKE. I think he ought to say he sorry first.

Low grey cloud. Rain. McKays went home and Eamonn too, with Amy who was driving that Morag's car. I cried, though no one saw.

Later he took Aunties to the station. Cried again. Why had I ever wanted empty house?

Grey. Rain. Very down. Rice pudding.

Grey. Rain. Miss Pincher in plastic hood and raincoat round, riding sit-up-and-beg bike, wanting to know if I'm ready to renew my contract.

Gave her coffee. She very nosey about the house, darting little glances everywhere. In the end I took her on guided tour.

I heard she lives in little terraced house in town with her old mother – and if Miss Pincher aged, how ancient must her old mother be?

Told her I wasn't at all sure about contract, and she said, 'Oh dear!' – and started looking round for coat.

Longing to ask her what known about that Todd.

'You must come back to us, you really must,' she goes. 'No Nursery Assistant, no proper care-taker . . .'

'No caretaker?'

'That dreadful man!' she says, lifting her hands.

'I know he's family, but he's just too much! You know he gave notice weeks and weeks ago – yes, he did, didn't you know? And yes, I will have just a little more cake. Thank you. But the plain fact of the matter is, though he pleaded domestic difficulties, the man's divorced. Oh, I'm aware of the attitude to divorce round here, and I'm not saying he doesn't share it, but the whole point is, he's not with his ex-wife. He simply can't be found. I've spoken to Pat on the telephone and she's of opinion – oh dear, should I be saying all this?'

I poured the old girl some more tea and handed her a plate of biscuits.

'Oh, yes, well, thank you. So – let us try to be charitable. Let us imagine that, as Pat seems to think, the man has gone down to London looking for work so that he may support his wife and child, not to mention Martha and – er – *her* baby. A little more milk, if I may . . .'

At least I didn't have a baby, I thought.

'Well, I must be going, I'm afraid,' the old dear said at last, having looked to see if any more cake and found that there wasn't. She rose reluctantly from a sea of cake crumbs like a greedy – who was that plump, nude bit who rode in on a sea shell holding her long hair so that you couldn't see her pussy? 'I do urge you to consider how much you're needed. And the – er – money, – er – useful, you know.'

She attacked her escaping wig, wrapped herself firmly in her coat, mounted her bicycle and left, those skinny legs in those thick woollen stockings propelling that crazy old bike.

He come in then. 'Who that?'

'Miss Pincher.'

186

'Oh.'

And he buggered off. No 'What she want?' or 'You going back there in the New Year?'

Nothing.

Said to him this morning as I was stripping Christmas tree, 'We talking yet?'

'I told you, I don't talk to tarts,' he said, and got behind *Daily Mail*.

Sod yer, as my old Mum used to say when the Rent Man coming and we hadn't got it.

New Year's Eve tomorrow.

Passed him in the hall just now carrying cup of tea and five sweetmeal digestives on a Willow Pattern plate. Brightened up immediately. Surely this means olive branch?

'Oh, Stanley, you shouldn't have!' I gushed.

'I didn't,' he said, passing on with the biscuits and tea into the lounge.

I just stared at him. Couldn't believe my ears. Sweetmeal digestives on a plate, and not for me . . .?

'Don't think I've forgotten you reading my book at Christmas Time!' I shouted after him. 'Because I haven't! What you want to go poking your big fat nose in it for, anyway?'

'Wanted to see if there was anything we could flog to Red, Red Roses,' he answered. 'On account of us being boracic lint with you spending and that Monkey House cum Gasworks down Westminster.'

'Me spending?' I called out. 'You know damn well you 'ad it right the second time and it's the Gumment.'

'I know it's the bloody Gumment,' he said slowly like someone speaking to idiot child. 'But it's you too. You're just not economical.'

187

I started to say, 'That's churches' but he interrupted.

'You're so wet where money's concerned you'd damp yer boots from the inside,' he went on, then he slammed the door. Fatgirl run out squawking, nearly lost half her tail.

Him and his digestives. Hope he chokes.

'We'd be alright if you got yourself a decent job!' I shouted. 'Instead of leaving it to me and a fancy money system!'

'You know I ain't been able to find one that pays and keep me pension!' he shouted back.

'You!' I said bitterly to myself. 'Couldn't find a knocking shop in Port Said!'

Got that one from Roderick.

Fatgirl come rubbing round me legs, and it come to me then that I didn't particularly like her, either. She only makes a fuss of me when she wants food — not like Plum, her mother, used to come to greet me at the gate, tail up in big hullo. All this one thinks about is if her belly full.

Fed up. Went to bed early.

New Year's Eve. Woke early, he not there. Found later he'd slept in spare room.

Rain coming in through hole in porch roof. Put bucket underneath. Plink! Plink-plink!

He got gardening book and huddled up all secretive by fire. Without people in it the house seems troubled now and — what's the word? *Alien.*

Nerves — mine — bristling with raw ends. Gotta do summing or I'll scream. And that cold wind blowing, found me out up here, nothing to do with the Force Nine gale outside. This is a peculiar and private chill, blows round me when I'm afraid I'm all alone.

Strikes me I spent a lot of me life in fear; illness, poverty, what the neighbours saying. Starts when you're small, dunnit, this fear of things? Another little baby come along and take your world away . . .

. . . even if nice when grownup, like Amy.

This cold wind was always blowing round me when he off with tart, even if he did pay all the bills.

Maybe the time has come to make a stand against this fear; I mean, he's sitting in there, got his brooding face on, exactly the same he had when he told me last time he wasn't coming back.

I should very much like to be the one that dished it out this time and not on the receiving end. I don't mean go off with someone, just be the one who left.

And too, they tell me that that Todd has gone to London.

Went upstairs. Checked my purse; £30 in notes and loose change, cheque card and old cheque book — he can have the new one come before Christmas — little blu pass book . . . well, I'll leave him that. Wouldn't be no use where I'm going, anyway.

Beautiful clothes, underclothes, night clothes, sponge bag and makeup things into holdall and little suitcase, one for either hand. Wait until I hear him go out to kitchen for fresh tea, then call taxi-rank at the station, using bedroom extension. Replace handset carefully in case it tings.

I read poem once in book Wayne leant me.

> This is the way the world ends
> Not with a bang but a whimper.

Can't remember who wrote it. It weren't H. Steiner-Rice.

Weren't Patience Strong, either – she all bright and telling everybody how to cope with life.

Not with a bang. That's true. We ain't had that for weeks and sodding weeks.

(Thirty quid. More'n enough to get me to Liverpool Street, then tube, then fast train from Victoria to Amy's. Think I can hear the taxi coming now.)

Not with a bang . . . Oh, he's a wimp, alright.

(It'll be good to be on the old Circle Line again.)

. . . *but a whimper.*

On the other hand, who's whimpering – now that she's going home?